A horn blared.

"That must be them now," said Chris. "Come on."

I followed her as she ran outside to the front of the house. A large white car with tail fins had pulled up at the curb. It had a bumper sticker saying Eat My Dust, Turkey. A brown plastic skull grinned at us from the rear window.

"It's the guys!" said Chris joyfully. "Fellas," she shouted, "here's my cousin Katy. She just got in this morning."

I couldn't understand why Chris seemed to think I'd be able to slip right into the group in her place. I wasn't at all sure this was the group I should be getting in with. I was not the sort of person who truly appreciated cars decorated with skulls. To put it plainly— skulls were not me.

Books by Janice Harrell

Puppy Love
Heavens to Bitsy
Secrets in the Garden
Killebrew's Daughter
Sugar 'n' Spice
Blue Skies and Lollipops
Birds of a Feather
With Love from Rome
Castles in Spain
A Risky Business
Starring Susy
They're Rioting in Room 32

JANICE HARRELL is the eldest of five children
and spent her high school years in the small,
central Florida town of Ocala. She earned her
B.A. at Eckerd College and her M.A. and Ph.D.
from the University of Florida. For a number of
years she taught English at the college level. She
now lives in North Carolina with her husband and
their young daughter.

JANICE HARRELL

They're Rioting in Room 32

Keepsake

FROM
CROSSWINDS

CROSSWINDS

New York • Toronto • Sydney
Auckland • Manila

First publication October 1987

ISBN 0-373-88009-X

RL 6.4, IL age 11 and up

Dear Reader:

Welcome to Crosswinds! We will be publishing four books a month, written by renowned authors and rising new stars. You will note that under our Crosswinds logo we are featuring a special line called Keepsake, romantic novels that are sure to win your heart.

We hope that you will read Crosswinds books with pleasure, and that from time to time you will let us know just what you think of them. Your comments and suggestions will help us to keep Crosswinds at the top of your reading list.

Nancy Jackson

Senior Editor
CROSSWINDS

Chapter One

But you said you'd be around to show me the ropes!'' I protested.

Chris threw a waterproof parka into her duffel bag. "No problem," she said. "You worry too much, did you know that?" She squinted critically at a pair of gypsy earrings and tossed them in after the parka.

"I still don't see why you can't wait another week before you go, the way you said you would."

"Look, it's Dad's idea to leave early, not mine. If I had any choice, do you think I'd be spending my junior year on a boat?"

Chris's parents had decided to sail around the world, living on their savings while getting away from the rat race. It sounded like fun and I might have liked to do it, too, except that my family didn't have a sail-boat. Also they didn't have any savings. For us, just paying for groceries had begun to look like a major challenge. My dad was officially out of a job, now that Bleeker Locks had decided to close down their entire Florida operation.

That was why, when Chris's dad, Uncle Henry, had offered to let Dad take over his job in the family company until he got back, Dad had jumped at the chance. The deal was that we were going to live in North Carolina, in Uncle Henry and Aunt Alice's house, feed the cat and water the philodendron until they finished sailing around the world.

I was thrilled about the whole idea. I knew I was ready for a bigger canvas than Pickipsee, Florida could offer me. I was doing a little reading in the works of Sigmund Freud, I had a subscription to *Psychology Today*, and when a show came on PBS called something like *The Brain*, I never missed it. This should give you the idea that I was not just fooling around with this stuff. I meant business. I was a serious student of the human mind. And Pickipsee Academy, with its tiny junior class made up of the same fifteen people I had known all my life, did not offer enough scope to a person with my interests. I needed to get to know new and different types—neurotics, psychopaths, obsessive types—the works. I had a feeling that Chris's school was just the laboratory of human behavior I had been looking for.

The only thing was, I really had been counting on Chris showing me around. I had been counting on it a lot.

I must have been making anxious whimpering noises because Chris went on, "The guys'll show you around. I already talked to them about it."

"What guys?"

She looked at me reproachfully as she rolled up three jerseys and stuffed them into a corner of the bag. "Bix, Mark and Fuzzy. I bet I've told you about them a hundred times, dodo. My best friends. My blood brothers. I told them that they're supposed to watch out for you while I'm gone. Listen, you're my legacy to those guys. They can watch out for you and you can watch out for them. Hampstead High isn't some namby pamby sweet little private school like that academy place you've been going to. Hampstead's the real world. It can be pretty cold and cruel. You're going to need friends."

"But what if these guys don't like me?"

"Like has nothing to do with it. You're my cousin, aren't you? I told them to look out after you, didn't I? Well, there you are. That's settled."

She zipped up the duffel bag with finality.

A horn blared outside.

"That must be them now," she said. "Come on."

I followed Chris as she ran outside to the front of the house. A large white car with tail fins had pulled up at the curb. It had a bumper sticker saying Eat My

Dust, Turkey. A brown plastic skull grinned at us from the rear window.

"It's the guys!" said Chris joyfully. "Fellas," she shouted, "here's my cousin Katy. She just got in this morning."

A door was flung open, some long legs in blue jeans appeared, and then the lean, handsome boy they belonged to unfolded himself and stood up. "This is Bix," Chris explained to me proudly. "The baddest guy in Hampstead."

Bix's ash-blond hair was short on top, longer and brushed back on the sides and he had light, amber-colored eyes, like a lynx. He was wearing a plain white shirt with a turned-up collar. Slung around the collar was a thin black tie dangling loose in front in a way disreputable enough to have earned ten demerits at Pickipsee Academy.

"Hey, Chrissie, baby," he said in a husky voice. "Tomorrow's the big day, huh?"

"I don't want to go!" wailed Chris. "You guys have gotta come with me, that's all."

A huge, bearlike guy in a black T-shirt got out of the car on the street side and stretched. "Don't I wish," he said lazily. He must have been all of six-foot-two, and though he wasn't exactly fat, he had the softly rounded look to his jawline of one who has loved pizzas and chocolate shakes from the cradle. He looked at me with gentle, curious eyes.

"The hulk over there is Mark," Chris told me. "If you need anybody to explain something to you, ask him. He knows just about everything."

Then the driver got out, a boy with straight mustard-colored hair, wearing a pair of ancient faded jeans that had a black bandanna tied around one knee. He leaned his skinny elbows on the car top and grinned at us.

"And that's Fuzzy," concluded Chris. "The gang's all here."

Well, I had wanted new and different types and these guys were certainly different. It hadn't quite soaked in on me until this moment that all of Chris's friends were boys. I mean, three boys is kind of a lot of boys at one time, if you aren't used to them. From a human behavior standpoint, getting to know them would no doubt prove very interesting, but from a personal standpoint it was a shade intimidating.

"We thought we'd all pile in and go cruising down Lakeside," said Fuzzy.

"Last time you'll get a chance for a while," Mark said. "Pile in Chris." He added, "And Katy, too, of course."

"Gee, guys," Chris said. "I can't. Dad made me promise I wouldn't go anywhere tonight because we've got to leave at six tomorrow morning."

"Six?" said Mark. "You must have got it wrong. The only thing people get up at six for is death by firing squad."

"Not much diff that I can see," said Chris. "I can't believe I'll be doing my junior year by correspondence course."

"You send us a post card from Tahiti," said Bix.

"I will," said Chris, as tears started welling up in her eyes.

"And don't go crying," said Fuzzy in alarm.

"I won't," promised Chris, swallowing hard. "Look, you guys, somebody's going to have to give Katy a ride to school tomorrow. She doesn't drive."

They all looked at me in blank astonishment and said in unison. "You don't drive?"

I could feel my face growing warm with embarrassment.

"No problem," Bix said after a moment's thought. "I'll teach her." I noticed that the others looked at each other a little oddly when he said that.

"Bix can drive, can't he?" I put in anxiously.

"Oh, he can *drive* all right," said Mark in funereal tones.

"Then it's all settled," said Bix. "We'll pick you up tomorrow at quarter of eight."

They climbed back into the car.

"Katy, you can go with them," said Chris. "You don't have to stay home just because I have to."

"Oh, that's all right," I said. "I think I'd better stand by in case you need me to help you finish packing. Or something."

Bix banged on the side of the car as the engine began to roar. "Bon voyage, Chrissie," Mark yelled. The

big white car coughed a little, then it sprinted away
down the street leaving a trail of black smoke.

"What's going on with you? Why didn't you want
to go?" Chris asked. "You know I've already finished packing. I don't need you to help."

"Those boys are perfect strangers to me."

"Don't be silly. I've known them since I was in the
third grade. They're a great bunch of guys."

Chris was acting as if she hadn't quite noticed that
she and I were two different people. It was true that we
looked sort of alike. We were both 5' 5" and we both
had short brown hair. We both had the short little
Callahan nose and we both had the Callahan determination. But there the similarity ended. Chris's idea
of fun was a big party; my idea of fun was a good
book. Chris liked skiing; I liked having both feet
planted solidly and safely on the ground. Chris was
one of those people who could never see what the
problem was; I actually liked working on problems. If
these boys had known Chris since the third grade, I
was sure they were going to be able to tell the differ-
ence between her and me. I couldn't understand why
she seemed to think I'd be able to slip right into the
group in her place.

There was another thing to consider. I wasn't at all
sure this was the group I should be getting in with. I
was not the sort of person who truly appreciated cars
decorated with skulls. To put it plainly—skulls were
not me.

However, for the immediate future, I was forced to admit I didn't have much choice in the matter. Except for my eight-year-old sister Caroline and my parents, to begin with I wasn't going to know a single other soul in town.

"That Bix is awfully good-looking," I said as we turned back toward the house.

"Yup," said Chris with pride. "Nobody's managed to break his nose yet."

"Why would anybody want to?" I said, looking at her oddly.

When she opened the front door I saw that Mom and Aunt Alice were huddled together over the dining-room table going over a list of crucial last-minute details such as when to feed the fish and how to unstop the garbage disposal, so I waited until we got back to Chris's room to continue the discussion. "What's this about somebody breaking Bix's nose?" I asked.

Chris sat down on the bed and looked at me seriously. "You're going to have to help the other guys keep an eye on Bix, Katy. He's kind of bad about getting into fights. It's not too much of a problem when you're at school because everybody there is really really careful to stay out of his way. It's when you're off somewhere and you run into kids from other schools that things can get sticky. If it looks like you're going to get into a fight type situation, my advice is that you slip the other guy a little hint about what he's up against. I mean, once the suckers realize that Bix is going to annihilate them, sometimes they just fade away, which is all for the best, believe me." She hugged herself and shuddered. "I hate blood," she said.

I couldn't have agreed with her more.

I cleared my throat. "That's very interesting," I said. "Where do you think he gets these unbridled aggressive instincts from? I mean, what do you think is going on with him?"

Chris shrugged. "He's always been that way. Everybody knows not to mess with Bix."

"You don't think there's any chance he would hit me, do you?"

"You? Don't be silly. You're a girl. Bix would never hit a girl."

I realized that there are times sexism can be useful. "Is there anything else I should know?"

"Well, Fuzzy isn't one of the world's great minds. You may have to repeat things for him, now and then," she admitted.

"What about that gigantic boy? Anything I should know about him?"

"Mark? You don't have to worry about Mark. He can take care of himself. Oh, gee, I wish I were staying home and you were sailing away in my place!" she said.

"So do I." I was conscious of an uneasy fluttering feeling in my stomach. For the first time I was wondering whether I was entirely up to broadening my horizons at Hampstead High.

Chris's family was ready right on schedule at six the next morning. Dad was going to drive them over to the coast where their schooner was waiting for them.

I threw a bathrobe over my nightgown and managed to drag myself outside to say goodbye. Everybody had gray faces in the dawn's early light, even Uncle Henry, who was brimming with enthusiasm. "'Oh, I must go down to the sea again,'" he said. "'To the lonely sea and the sky/ And all I ask is a...'"

"Henry," said Aunt Alice, "you didn't forget to pack your allergy pills, did you?"

"I won't need them. There isn't any ragweed growing out there on the high seas."

Uncle Henry got in the front seat of the car next to Dad. "Let's go, Alice," he said. "Time and tide wait for no man."

"The plunger is in the hall closet," Aunt Alice called to Mom. "I forgot to mention that we've been having a little trouble with the drain in the master bathroom."

"Good luck, Katy," Chris called. "I'll write."

Mom and I waved as they drove off. "Well, honeybunch," she said, putting her arm around me, "we're on our own now." Mom was smiling. As for me, something basic seemed to have happened to my self-confidence and I thought I would save the smiles until I was sure I would survive the entry into Hampstead High.

Chapter Two

I was surprised that Mark was alone when he came by to pick me up for school. He drove up in a classic blue Studebaker that looked as if it had been lovingly restored with fifteen coats of lacquer. It came to a stop in front of my house and stood there in the sunshine, sort of shimmering with perfection. "Bix forgot he had preschool detention," Mark explained when I climbed into the front seat beside him.

"What did he get preschool detention for?" I asked, not sure that I wanted to know.

"He shoved Billy Tyler over the banisters in the east wing. Billy told Coach it was an accident and not Bix's fault. But Coach said he'd give him detention anyway to remind him not to have any more accidents. I tell you, it's getting plain dangerous to be around Bix. I've never seen him in this kind of shape. Since he's gotten this thing for Celia Morrison, he goes around all the time just hoping he'll find somebody dumb enough to fight him.''

I felt at once that my subtle understanding of human behavior might prove useful with this problem. "Isn't there anything anybody can do?" I asked.

He grinned. "Talk to Celia? Tell her to give him a break? Not likely. Hey, has anybody ever told you that you look sort of like Chris?"

"Just the nose," I said.

"I think you're right. It's the nose. It gives you this look of a very expensive cat. One of those with fluffy hair. Maybe a Persian. You know the kind of cat I mean?"

"Actually, I'm more a dog person," I said. "Is Hampstead a very hard school, do you think?"

"The hardest part is keeping sane," he said, turning onto a broad avenue. "You've got to remember that all the people here wish they were somewhere else and that makes them go a little crazy at times. Mrs. Wiggins, my English teacher, wishes she were in Paris writing the great American novel. Coach Mather wishes he were playing for the Boston Red Sox. I wish I were at the beach. Bix wishes he were at war. I take that back, Bix *is* at war. But anyway, I am forced to admit that Hampstead is a weird place. The trick in surviving is you just can't take it seriously. That's all there is to it. And speaking of school, that's it up ahead.''

I could see that the high school, at the foot of the hill, was a series of one- and two-story buildings set back on several acres of green lawn with a football field and a baseball diamond laid out to one side of it. Cars seemed to be careening in all directions on the street in front of the place and huge numbers of kids were milling around the buildings, looking from the distance like a tide of red, yellow and blue specks of color.

When we got up closer to the school, Mark turned onto the street just east of the school complex and drove into a parking lot labeled Juniors Only. Stickers Required. This was a parking lot that gave a whole new meaning to the word congested. It was incredibly full of people and cars and as we entered, Mark had to slow to about four mph. All of a sudden someone banged on my car door with an open hand. I jumped so high my head nearly hit the top of the car. Fuzzy's grinning face appeared at the window. "Chris get off okay?'' he yelled.

"Fine,'' I called back.

"Get your lousy hands off the car, Fuzz,'' Mark yelled.

Fuzzy grinned an apology and taking out a handkerchief ostentatiously polished off his hand prints.

The Studebaker crept onward. At last Mark spotted an open parking place and snapped into it with the speed of a laser beam.

Bells were ringing from six directions when I opened the car door. When I got out I found myself being swept along with a mob of kids moving away from the parking lot.

"Meet you at the car after school," Mark yelled through cupped hands. After that I couldn't hear much of anything except the loud electric clangor of the bells on the buildings nearest me.

When I found my way to the office I got signed up for my classes with no trouble. That was the easy part. The hard part was going to be getting used to all the people. The student handbook said there were fifteen hundred kids at Hampstead High, but I felt sure the officials were hiding something, like maybe that a nasty accident in the chemistry lab had resulted in the cloning of those original fifteen hundred. In support of this theory, I can only say that to me a lot of those kids looked alike.

Hampstead High was crowded. I mean we're talking major crowded. We're talking half-price-sale-in-Calcutta type crowded. I got the feeling that if I tripped during the between-classes stampede, I would have been trampled by thousands of high tops and swept up by the evening cleaning crew.

And the worst part was I didn't know anybody. I wondered why it hadn't occurred to me that not knowing anybody at school was going to be horrible. By the end of third period I began to have the feeling that I would never see another familiar face. Just then, in the hallway of the west wing, I heard Bix yelling, "Katy!"

In his effort to get my attention, he had bumped into a brown-haired guy with glasses. The guy bent over to get his books, muttering, "My fault. Sorry about that, Bix. Extremely sorry about that."

I noticed that a path quickly cleared for Bix as he moved over to speak to me. "How's it going?" he asked me. "Got any good classes?"

"It looks like it's going to be very challenging," I said. "I think I can say that much. I'm going to have to give a lot of thought to whether I can possibly catch up in chemistry or whether I should just fake it."

"Fake it," advised Bix. "Say, we gotta get on with those driving lessons of yours. Maybe Saturday, okay? I'll call you."

As he moved away, a strange person with a shaved head and an earring made of feathers brushed against him, and I heard the guy saying, "Oops, sorry, Bix. My mistake. Entirely my mistake!"

I wished I had thought to question Chris closely about Bix's driving. Exactly what was so sinister about it? Maybe I should ask Dad if he'd be willing to try again at teaching me. The problem was that ever since that first lesson when I had begun by backing into our neighbor's new Plymouth, Dad had said that I was just going to have to wait another year until his and Mom's nerves were in better shape before they could give me any driving lessons. I was not too hopeful of getting them to change their minds.

The next period, fourth, was English class, my favorite subject. I had always made A's in English, so after I found the classroom, I took a seat on the third row expecting to enjoy myself. The teacher, Mrs. Wiggins, had the pale skin and the perfect subject-verb agreement typical of English teachers, but she also had laugh lines in the corners of her eyes, and I was hopeful that she might have a sense of humor.

The day's class turned out to be a lecture about Byron and Shelley and Keats and others of that ilk, which was interesting, but then Mrs. Wiggins looked at her watch and said, "As I promised you, class, today I will allow you to use the last ten minutes of class for a short debate on a topic that has lately become of great concern here at Hampstead." She wrote on the board—"Resolved: the football field should be turned into a rice paddy."

At first I thought it was a joke, but I looked around and nobody was laughing. Everyone was acting as if Mrs. Wiggins had been perfectly serious about the rice paddies. Rice paddies? She *had* to be kidding. But there was no doubt that the topic was generating more excitement than Byron and Shelley had. I could almost feel the class's motor revving up as kids sat up straighter in their seats and looked expectantly at the podium.

A thin boy with a prominent Adam's apple got up, placed a sheaf of notes on the podium and began to argue the pro side of the rice paddy question. He had a number of good arguments. He pointed out that students working in the rice paddies would be learning marketable agricultural skills, that the rice could be sold to make much needed improvements in the school like additional parking lots (cheers from the class), and that furthermore the rice paddies would serve a useful purpose by helping feed the world's hungry people. We all applauded enthusiastically when he sat down.

Next came a guy whose shoulders were so big it looked as if he might be hiding a couple of hams under his green school sweater. Putting his notes on the podium, he gave the class a toothy smile as a preface. I noticed he had large teeth. I'm not sure what he planned to say then because a handful of rice suddenly landed right in his face. Then, all at once kids began producing bags of rice from their desks and started throwing it all over the place. It was raining rice. I combed it out of my hair with my fingers, then a pebbly handful hit me on the ear. Over by the pencil sharpener, the guy with the big shoulders had picked up the skinny boy with the Adam's apple and was shaking him the way a terrier shakes a favorite plastic toy.

After I had dumped a few grains of rice out of my shoe, I looked up at the front of the class and I saw that Mrs. Wiggins did not look happy. She had her arms folded, and her eyes were cold. A lot of whistling and shouting went on while the rice lasted, but in the nature of things, it wasn't long before people started running out of rice and soon silence fell on the class. Then Mrs. Wiggins spoke.

"Joshua," she said, "you may go to the office and ask permission to bring back some brooms from the maintenance room."

"But Mrs. Wiggins," he protested. "I won't have time to get back before lunch."

"Isn't it lucky we have all this rice, then," she said sweetly. "None of you need starve. Celia and Katy, the innocent parties, may go on to lunch. The rest of you will remain here to assist Joshua in the cleanup."

When Celia and I left, the rest of the class were down on their hands and knees grubbing at grains of rice with their fingernails.

"I guess I've led a pretty sheltered life," I commented as we moved in the direction of the lunchroom. "I've never been in a rice riot before."

She smiled, revealing a dimple. She was a slender girl with a heart-shaped face and wavy blond hair down to her waist. "I never have, either," she said. "Actually, the kids called me and told me to bring some rice, so I knew what was going to happen, but I can't afford to get involved in that kind of thing. I have more important things to do." She shrugged. "Demonstrations are okay for people who need a hobby, I guess."

"Demonstrations? You mean, they're actually serious about turning the football field into a rice paddy?"

"Well, I haven't seen anybody working up cost projections on keeping the football field flooded or anything like that, if that's what you mean. I think they're just making an antifootball statement."

"I guess I shouldn't make snap judgments, but isn't Hampstead a kind of unusual school?"

"You think?" she asked, looking at me with intelligent interest. "I've kind of wondered about that myself. A lot of the things people do around here don't seem to make much sense, but I figure there must be some reason why they act that way."

"Acting out unconscious motives," I said. "That's what it is. Have you read any Freud?"

"Are you reading Freud?" she asked. I was pleased to see she looked impressed.

When we reached the cafeteria, we shoved the doors open and went in to join the line.

"Well, I've started *The Interpretation of Dreams*," I said. "Every morning I try to write down my dreams as soon as I wake up. Freud says that's the best way to study them. Of course, with us moving up here and all, I've kind of gotten behind with it."

"I guess it must be tough coming in new and not knowing anybody," she said.

"I have met a few boys," I said. "Do you know Fuzzy Wallace, or Mark Metcalf or Bix Bixby?"

Her expression stiffened. "Oh, yes, I know them."

"They seem to be nice," I said hopefully.

"Very nice," she said in a distant voice.

At first, I couldn't think of what I had done wrong, but then I suddenly remembered what had seemed vaguely familiar about this girl. Her name was Celia. I had just heard somebody talking about a Celia that morning. This must be the girl that Bix was so totally gone on.

"Do you belong to any school clubs?" I asked. "I've been wondering if I should join some. To get to know people."

"I belong to the Latin club," she said. "But I haven't been able to get to any meetings this year. Between schoolwork and my flute practice, there isn't much time left for anything else. Some people around here don't understand that when a person has serious goals, that person is not going to waste her time going to meetings, or cruising on Lakeside Avenue or hanging around Brendles."

"Oh, I understand perfectly," I said quickly. "I've always had serious goals. I want to be a psychologist or a psychiatrist someday so I don't let anything keep me away from my schoolwork."

"Friendship is one thing," Celia went on. "But it's a mistake to get into some big romance with a boy and let yourself get distracted from what really matters. I've got a flute audition for the Allstate Band coming up in February, and I need total concentration if I'm going to have a good chance at one of those first three chairs. People around here don't seem to know what it's like to have ambition and talent."

"Oh, I agree entirely," I said. "Absolutely. Too many girls act as if boys are the only thing that matters. They just go berserk if some really good-looking boy comes along, somebody like—just for an example—Bix."

She grabbed a tray and threw some silverware on it. "And if I were going to get involved with a boy, which I'm not, the very last kind of boy I would get involved with is a boy who is still getting into fights. At his age it's ridiculous."

I picked up my meatballs and spaghetti in thoughtful silence. Celia had gotten herself pretty steamed up and I was not surprised when she strode off without inviting me to sit with her. I was, however, a little disappointed. It looked like a cold, unfriendly world of strangers out there in the cafeteria.

"Katy!" someone called. I turned and spotted Fuzzy, Bix and Mark sitting together. Mark beckoned me to join them. I felt a rush of gratitude that Chris had left me as a legacy to her gang. It was certainly a relief to see some friendly, familiar faces.

As soon as I sat down, Bix fixed me with those amber-colored eyes of his. "I didn't know you knew Celia," he said in a voice vibrant with emotion.

I hastily popped a meatball in my mouth. "She's in my English class," I said, eager to change the subject to something less inflammatory. "You'll never believe what happened in there today," I said. "Everybody started throwing rice around!"

"The rice paddy controversy again, I see," said Mark. "Was this Mrs. Wiggins's class? Who spoke for the pro side?"

"Some skinny guy with an Adam's apple," I said.

"Ernie Findlater," said Fuzzy promptly. "He's real smart. I bet he was good. Every time I see him lately, if he's waiting for the bus or even if he's eating lunch, he's reading some book about rice."

"Actually, he's eating the books," said Mark. "That's why he seems so smart. They're processed directly in the brain."

"No joke?" said Fuzzy, looking startled.

Bix leaned over the table toward me and said softly, "Did Celia mention me?"

"Not exactly," I said, my eyes shifting wildly as I thought of some escape. "Actually, we were talking about ambition and how a girl shouldn't get involved with a boy because it's too distracting."

Bix made some sound low in his throat that sounded sort of like "Aaaargh," swept his tray off the table and got up.

He stepped right into the path of a blond boy trying to return his tray and knocked him flat. A dribble of milk from the almost empty carton trickled in a narrow white path on the grimy floor.

"Hey, you ran right into me, fella," the victim yelped, straightening his glasses.

Bix gently helped him up. "If you'd be interested in making something of it," he said. "I'd be happy to meet you after school."

At this, the blond boy's vision seemed to clear. "No, no," he said. "Sorry, my fault. I've always been clumsy. That's what my father's always saying, 'Michael, you are clumsy to a fault, you nitwit.' Sorry. Guess I'd better be off now."

He beat a quick retreat to the garbage bins, and Bix, his prey out of reach, was left standing over the spilled milk. We were all relieved when he turned and stalked out of the cafeteria.

"Whew," I said.

Mark began on his second dessert. "I know it doesn't matter to Bix—he doesn't care if he ever eats—but I think all these scenes are bad for the digestion."

"I don't think he's ever going to get anywhere with Celia," I said. "She works all the time. And besides, she's totally repelled by the way he gets into fights."

"She told you that?" said Mark, lifting a forkful of cake.

"She was vehement." I leaned on my elbows and thought a minute. "Of course, on the bright side, you know the psychologists tell us that hate is not the opposite of love, indifference is. Maybe there's something we can do to help Bix."

Mark eyed me warily. "I think it's better to let people handle their own lives," he said.

"We need to figure out a way to stop him from fighting," I said.

"Ain't no way," said Fuzzy.

"People have been using the wrong approach, that's all," I said. "When Coach Mather gave him detention for pushing Billy, that was an example of the wrong approach. It's a well-known fact that it doesn't do as much good to punish for bad behavior as it does to reward for good behavior. Behavioral psychologists use what is called 'positive reinforcement.' You see, every time somebody does what they're supposed to, you immediately give them a small reward, like an M & M. You give them an M & M every time they do what they're supposed to and before you know it you've got a changed person.''

Fuzzy's brow was furrowed with concentration. ''You mean, every time Bix *doesn't* want to fight, we give him an M & M?''

''That's right,'' I said. ''That's the idea!'' I was encouraged that Fuzzy had caught on so fast.

Fuzzy bit into a roll. ''Won't work then. Bix always wants to fight.''

''Fuzzy's got a point,'' said Mark. ''Besides, for Bix, the fight is the reward. He likes fighting *better* than M & M's.''

Behind us, someone fell against a table. This was not surprising. Collisions were inevitable in a place as crowded as Hampstead High. But I was jumpy and wheeled around in my chair. At the table behind me, I saw six or seven guys wearing matching green windbreakers. The guy in the middle, a tall brunette with smooth hair, was looking at the toppled salt shaker on the table with an expression of horror. As I watched, he picked up the salt shaker gingerly, as if he expected it to explode, and threw some salt over his shoulder.

"Did you see that?" I said, turning back to Mark and Fuzzy. "That guy throwing salt over his shoulder?"

Mark glanced up. "Peyton Richardson," he said. "The mayor's son. I guess he's superstitious."

"You see the jackets?" Fuzzy said. "Kinda neat, huh? They call themselves 'the Paladins.' If you look real close, you can see there's a knight in armor on the emblems they sewed on the jackets."

"Are they a gang?" I asked, sneaking another glance behind me.

"More like a fraternity," said Mark. "They elect people in by secret ballot. I think they sit around a lot talking about who's good-looking and who's popular and other such intellectually stimulating topics. There's a school rule against fraternities, but somehow it never gets invoked against the Paladins."

"Influence," said Fuzzy darkly.

"Well, that business with the salt just goes to show how irrational people are," I said. "Think of all the people who won't walk under a ladder! The mind is pretty primitive. And, you know, when I look at it that way, it seems as if it ought to be easy to change Bix's behavior. If I just knew how to go about it." I stared thoughtfully at my milk carton. "I wonder if Freud has anything to say about fist fights."

Chapter Three

Bix gave me my first driving lesson on Saturday. I was glad to see that he drove what looked like a simple sedan. Its rear end seemed to be jacked up a little higher than usual, and its tires looked overly large, but at least there were no skulls in the windows.

As we drove off, he reached up and prodded at the car top. "Feel that?" he asked. "That's a roll bar. I had it put in specially. That way if it rolls over, the top doesn't cave in."

I clutched at the arm rest. I didn't understand why a car would want to roll over and I felt at once that it wasn't a very good idea.

"It's a safety measure," he said. "We're heading out to my Uncle Dan's farm. You never see any cops out there and Uncle Dan's got a lot of private dirt roads you can practice on.''

As we got out in the country, he picked up speed. "You hear people say 'Speed kills,'" he said. "Not true. It's bad driving that kills. You've got to be on your toes, think ahead, keep both hands on the wheel. Never drive unless your reflexes are in good shape. Now watch me take this corner up ahead. There are a few technical points you should notice. Here we go— I hit the brakes, then trail off. I pivot my foot, tap the accelerator with the heel, double clutch and down-shift. Now I roll the wheel over and at the apex of the corner I drift over to the exit point." When he had finished turning and we were on the straightaway, he said, "Now I'm all set up for the next corner, see?" He looked over at me and smiled.

I would normally have smiled back. But I couldn't. My face was frozen with fear. I had never turned a corner so fast before.

He slowed the car down and pulled off on a shoulder. I saw that we were now on a deserted stretch of road. The only vehicle in sight was a distant tractor moving in a cloud of dust. I was glad to see that there were at least some signs of life, however far away. If the car took it in its head to go rolling over, at least there would be someone around to pull us out of the wreckage. I began to wonder if I really wanted to learn how to drive, after all.

Bix got out of the car and came around to my side. "Okay, you try now," he said.

I reminded myself that if I didn't learn to drive soon, people were going to start mistaking me for a sophomore. I forced myself to slide over behind the steering wheel. Bix got in and fastened his seat belt. We sat there a moment in silence. "Well, what are you waiting for?" he asked.

"I was hoping you'd explain how to turn the thing on," I said meekly.

He looked at me aghast, but then pulled himself together. "Okay, we start at the beginning," he said. He patted the dashboard. "What we have here is a car, c-a-r," he said.

It wasn't exactly a promising beginning, but Bix was not the type to get discouraged. Slowly he showed me how to turn the thing on and how to manage the clutch. I choked the car down ten or twenty times before I finally got it in gear and rolling. I then celebrated this progress by grinding the gears. Next I got the clutch and the brake mixed up and stopped so fast that only the seat belts saved us from being plastered against the windshield. After I recovered from that little difficulty, I was tooling along at a madly risky twenty miles an hour when I got rattled and ran the car right off the road, narrowly missing a ditch. None of this bothered Bix. Although it must have been clear to him that when it came to driving a car I was not what they call a natural, he did not seem discouraged and at the end of an hour, I had actually taken the car all the way down the road and turned around. I was driving!

And the really nice thing was that not once during the entire lesson did Bix suffer from the whitened knuckles and the sharply sucked in breath that seemed to hit Dad whenever I approached the ignition. Of course, what I realized was that Bix had one tremendous advantage over Dad as an instructor. He didn't know the meaning of fear.

I thought about how surprised my parents would be when one of these days I announced that I had learned how to drive and was ready to get my license. Bix got back in the driver's seat and turned the car in the direction of home.

"Have you seen Celia around lately?" he asked with studied casualness.

"Not this week. She's been awfully busy. But we're supposed to get together to study chemistry next week. I'm hoping I can get to know her better."

"She's an angel," he breathed. "She's like a flower. Do you know what I mean? A lily, maybe. Or one of those flowers that grows up in the mountains away from all the litter and stuff. It's like she's a princess from another world, someone very special. There's nobody like her, Katy, nobody."

At least it was clear where he stood. I eyed him warily. "She's great, all right," I said. "But are you sure she's for you?"

He gave me a searing look.

"I mean, the girl hates violence," I went on quickly. "She thinks getting into fights is childish. This may not be a match made in heaven."

To my alarm, we began picking up speed. "You're acting like I spend my life beating little kids' heads against the cement," he said between clenched teeth. "I've never been in a fight without some good reason. Anyway, not lately."

"Right," I said hastily. "Of course." It was pretty clear he couldn't be talked out of his devotion to Celia. I knew a lost cause when I saw one. I would have to think of some other way to approach Bix's problem.

On Monday, Mark drove me to school again because Bix was still serving early detention and Fuzzy lived in the other direction from us. That was fine with me. Of the three boys, Mark was easily the one I liked best to talk to. He was one of the few people I had ever met with whom the opener "Have you read any good books lately?" could actually lead to an interesting conversation.

"How did the driving lesson go?" he asked.

"I'm making progress," I said. "Why didn't you warn me about Bix's driving?"

"What could I say? You can't say he's not a good driver, because he is. You can't even really say he's not a safe driver because he's never had an accident, never had a moving violation, even."

"Well, you could say his driving contributes in a major way to heart failure. I think you could say that."

He smiled. "Yeah, I guess so. It's just the way Bix is." He looked at me out of the corner of his eye. "You like him?"

"Sure, I like him," I said.

"Most girls do," sighed Mark.

"Not Celia."

"Ah, well, that's Bix all over. It's not enough that he bowls over every girl he meets. He's got to go after some blinking Holy Grail or something. You know those guys that call themselves the Paladins, Peyton Richardson's bunch? They aren't really like the noble knights of yore the way they'd like to think. They're just a bunch of clothes-happy jerks. It's Bix that's the paladin. The only trouble is that being a paladin can be inconvenient in the modern world."

We were coming down the hill toward the school and I noticed right away that something was going on. Over on the east side of the school where there should have been an expanse of grass, I could see a vast pool of water reflecting the light. A police car was pulled up in front of the administration building.

"Look!" I said.

"Good grief," said Mark softly. "They've opened the fire hydrant and flooded the football field."

"Why would anybody do anything like that?"

We were now turning off the avenue and heading toward the parking lot. "I have a feeling this is the latest move of the pro rice paddy party," Mark said.

It turned out he was right. After the bell rang for assembly, when we all filed into the auditorium, I noticed a clutch of kids in the back wearing coolie hats and broad smiles. I was pretty sure they were the ones responsible for the flooding.

The lights in the auditorium switched off and the stage lights came on. A nervous-looking student came out, stood in front of the footlights and announced that the scheduled assembly topic "Safety at School" had been scrapped because the principal, Mr. Alvin Jones, was going to give a special address.

There was a wave of movement behind me as the coolie hats were swept off heads and stashed under folding seats. Mr. Jones strode out on the stage. He was wearing a dark business suit. He did not look much over forty to me, but he was completely gray. It seemed quite possible that being principal of Hampstead had done that to him.

"Vandalism will not be tolerated," he snarled at the microphone. "When the perpetrators of this infantile deed are identified, and I must tell you that the police are even now pursuing this matter, they will be punished to the full extent of the law." He began to gesture like a television evangelist, reaching his left arm high as if he were planning to pull down the curtains. "Furthermore," he said, "I wish to go on record as giving you warning that no infractions of the rules will be tolerated in any way. Today, it's stealing pencil erasers, tomorrow it's organized crime." He twisted his whole body in a half pirouette and brought his arm down decisively. "This lawlessness must be nipped in the bud!" he said, his voice rising.

The boy to my left was regarding him dispassionately with folded arms. "He moves good," he commented.

"No more Mr. Nice Guy," snarled Mr. Jones, pointing a finger in our direction. "You want to break a rule, kids? Go ahead. Make my day!"

There was a scattering of applause as he hunched his shoulders and retired from the stage, but I could not tell whether the appreciation was for the sentiment or the choreography.

I saw no further sign of the kids in the coolie hats, and I fancied there was a certain subdued quality about the student body as we filed out, but I was not particularly concerned. After all, I was not a member of the rice paddy party. Furthermore, I had no plans to steal pencil erasers.

That afternoon, after school, I made my way to the parking lot, as usual, to meet Mark at the car. I had a little trouble getting by on the sidewalk because a crowd was gathering. I tried to make my way around it, but then I realized that people all around me were saying "Fight!" "Come on. It's a fight!"

As the significance of these words sank in on me, my blood ran cold. I began clawing my way up to the front of the crowd. By sheer determination, I soon reached the inside rung of the wide circle that had been cleared for the combatants. Just as I had feared, Bix was in the center of the circle. He had his fists up and he looked very happy, even radiant. Facing him, in a green windbreaker, was Peyton Richardson, his face white. I had the feeling he was already regretting whatever it was that had brought him to this pass.

"Want to tell everybody that you're slime, Richardson?" asked Bix menacingly.

Peyton's answer was a quick swipe at Bix's face. But Bix danced aside and the blow missed him. While Peyton was off balance, Bix clipped him playfully on his ear and smiled, a look of pure joy. Peyton, enraged, lunged at him. Bix dodged, and when Peyton, looking confused, came at him again, Bix brought his fist up under Peyton's chin with a loud crack. Peyton seemed for a millisecond to float there, then, blood trickling from his mouth, he toppled to the ground.

A sort of sigh went up from the crowd and three boys in green jackets rushed out and bent over Peyton. He seemed to be trying weakly to fight them off, so at least he wasn't unconscious.

"Fight!" somebody yelled in the distance. "It's a fight, Mr. Jones."

Fuzzy, Mark and I ran to Bix. "You gotta get out of here quick, Bix," Mark rumbled softly. "Jones is on the way."

I grabbed Bix's hand and pulled him in the direction of the car. A second later all four of us were running full speed for the Studebaker. When we got to the car, breathless, Mark practically picked Bix up and threw him in back. Fuzzy jumped in with Bix, Mark and I got in the front seat, then we took off. I could hear Bix in back, down on the floor, laughing.

"Keep him down, man," Mark growled to Fuzzy. "Now I'm going to take it really slow getting out of here. We don't want to look suspicious." The car moved slowly out of the parking lot. I glanced anxiously over at the crowd, which was now dispersing. I could see a man in a dark business suit with a clump of kids gathered around him. I shivered.

"Do you think anybody's going to tell him who was fighting?" I asked.

"I don't think so," said Mark, obviously trying to sound optimistic. "It was a fair fight and everybody knows they can't lock Bix up the rest of his life. I think they'll be afraid that if he found out who squealed on him he'd go after them."

When we had gotten about a block away from the school, Mark stopped the car. "Okay, Fuzzy," he said. "You go get Bix's car. Get his car first and then go back later and get yours. If anybody sees you, just say you forgot you brought your car to school and so you got a ride home and then had to come back for it." There was a jangling noise as Bix tossed his keys to Fuzzy.

Fuzzy got out and slunk away, looking like someone hired by the CIA when it was suffering from budget cuts.

"That's okay, then," sighed Mark. "The beauty of it is Fuzzy can say something dumb like that he forgot he drove his car to school and everybody will believe him."

"Hey, when can I get up?" asked Bix. "I'm getting a crick in my neck."

"You can get up when I say, man," said Mark. "What do you think you were doing out there? You want to get yourself kicked out of school?"

"That's negative reinforcement, Mark," I murmured. "Total waste of time."

"That scumball insulted the woman I love," said Bix stiffly.

I peered over the back seat. "Really? What did he say?"

"It's not fit for a girl's ears," said Bix.

"Honestly, talk about medieval," I said. "How am I going to learn about human behavior if I don't get to hear what scumballs say?"

"Drop it, Katy," said Mark. "It doesn't matter. Okay, you can get up now, Bix. What I don't understand is, if Peyton insulted Celia why can't you let Celia be the one to whop him?"

I looked at him approvingly. "That makes sense to me," I said.

"That's dumb," said Bix. "Girls don't fight." He added sullenly, "Besides, she didn't hear what he said."

"He was just baiting you, you know that?" said Mark.

"Well, he got what he was asking for," said Bix. He sat back and folded his arms, his amber eyes glowing.

I personally did not think it was likely that Peyton had been deliberately baiting Bix. After all, the guy might be slime, but we had no reason to think he was suicidal.

Probably he was just one of those types that lean against the corners of buildings and make personal remarks when girls pass by —your basic unredeemed male chauvinist pig. I had often had the impulse to clobber those types myself so even though I deplore violence, I could not be entirely down on Bix for socking him.

"You don't think Peyton will squeal, do you?" I asked, suddenly uneasy.

Mark rolled his eyes. "That'll be all we need. Anybody can see that Jones is just looking for somebody to make an example of, and I don't have to tell you what your dad's going to say if you get thrown out of school, Bix." Mark explained to me, "The Reverend Mr. Bixby is one of the leading believers in the turn-the-other-cheek approach."

I hadn't realized that Bix was a preacher's kid. Given Bix's disposition I could certainly see how it could make for awkwardness.

I turned around. "By any chance are you adopted, Bix?"

He shook his head, but he was beginning to look troubled. I could see he didn't like the idea of his father finding out about what had just happened.

"Your father would be really mad, huh?" I said.

"Worse than that," said Bix. "He'd be grieved." He groaned. "Look, Metcalf, he threw the first punch. I got a hundred witnesses. If he squeals on me he gets thrown out, too, right?"

Clearly, Bix had not heard about people turning state's evidence.

"Look," I said. "Let's not get overly worried about this. The chances are nothing will come of it at all."

But that was where I was wrong.

Chapter Four

The next day I happened to be behind Peyton Richardson in a line to the water fountain. I recognized him right away even from the back because of his distinctive green windbreaker and his very smooth dark hair, which had been saturated with mousse until it had the consistency of plastic. He bent over and turned on the spray of water. The water spurted up and sloshed over his mirrored sunglasses and his nose. This was not Peyton's week, obviously.

He straightened up, wincing slightly as a bruised muscle protested. Then he removed his sunglasses and wiped them on his jeans and I saw that he had two black eyes. He looked like a raccoon. I hadn't known that a blow to the jaw could do that. He must have banged his nose when he fell after Bix hit him. He swiftly replaced the sunglasses, then turned and looked full at me without recognizing me. I realized, with relief, that he had no idea I was one of Bix's crowd. Of course, he hadn't been in much shape to notice anybody when I last saw him.

"Move it, Richardson," snarled the boy behind me in line. "You think we got all day?"

Peyton flushed slightly and stepped out of the way. As I bent over the water fountain, he ambled away nonchalantly to join the other boys in the green windbreakers who were standing next to the wall of the locker room. All of them were standing in exactly the same way, with their weight on the right leg, the left leg thrust forward, thumbs hooked in their jeans pockets and shoulders slumped. I could imagine them gathering over at Peyton's house and practicing looking cool in front of a full-length mirror. "Okay, fellows, all together now, let's *stand*."

As I left the water fountain, I walked over right next to the guys in the green windbreakers, but though my nervous system kept giving off alarmed flight-fight signals like a demented videogame, they didn't seem to notice me.

"He's going to be sorry," Peyton was saying in a low voice. "He's going to be pretty sick that he tangled with me, I can tell you."

Peyton was not looking toward the guy in the water line as he spoke. He was staring blankly at a painted concrete-block wall, and judging by his tone of voice, he was seeing Bix's image on that wall as clearly as if it were being beamed there by a film projector. I suppose he was thinking that it was because Bix had leveled him that he couldn't get respect in the water line anymore.

I would have liked to hang around to see if he said anything else, but just then the bell went off and I had to run to my next class.

At lunchtime, I went over to sit with Fuzzy and Mark as usual. I put my tray down and scanned the table with alarm. "Where's Bix?" I asked quickly. "Is something the matter?"

Mark pushed my chair out for me with one foot. "He'll be along. No problem."

Sure enough, Bix came walking through the double doors of the cafeteria a minute later. He had a way of looking as if he had spent the morning strolling the boulevards of Paris instead of just slogging away at English and algebra like the rest of us. He spotted us and smiled as he got into the lunch line.

I knew that I was biased in Bix's favor on account of his being so sweet and patient with me while I was trying to learn to drive, but still I just could not see how Celia could resist that smile. Here was a guy who looked as if he'd stepped out of one of those racy jeans ads, a guy who would have been perfectly cast in some film that called for the movie star to turn into a cougar during the full moon. And yet Celia kept saying her flute was more interesting than he was. That didn't make sense. It was true that Bix did not happen to turn my knees to butter, but they would never have used his type to sell jeans if mine had been the typical reaction.

As I turned to open my milk carton and my eye fell on Mark and Fuzzy—no beauties, but a great pair of guys—it hit me how empty Hampstead High would have seemed to me without them. I wanted them to be happy always. I couldn't stand it that Bix kept getting himself into messes. The fact was that underneath my sharp, incisive mind and my scientific interest in human behavior was a heart as sentimental as Louisa May Alcott's.

"Mark," I said nervously, "what if all those guys in the green windbreakers gang up on Bix and jump him?"

Fuzzy grinned. "Heck, they aren't going to do a thing like that."

"You mean, you and Mark could beat them? There are at least six of them, I think."

"That's not what Fuzzy means," Mark said. "I guess if it came to that I could knock a few heads together, even though when it comes to fighting I am strictly a civilian. And Fuzzy could bite their knee-caps, couldn't you, Fuzz?" he said, giving Fuzzy a playful shove. "But the point is, how would something like that make them look?"

"Like creeps, that's what," Fuzzy chortled.

"You see, Katy," Mark said indulgently, "some things are just not done."

I was relieved to hear it. There had been times since my arrival at Hampstead High when it had seemed to me that almost anything could be done. I would not have been surprised to find kids practicing voodoo in the washrooms.

Mark looked at me sympathetically. "Don't worry about Bix. He'll be okay."

Bix brought his tray over to the table and sat down. "Well, you guys going to the Mozart festival tonight?"

"The Mozart festival?" I said.

"Yeah. The flute choir is doing a salute to Mozart."

"That sounds very interesting," I said. "Maybe I will go."

"I didn't know you liked classical music, Katy," said Mark, giving me a curious look.

"I think we all ought to try to expose ourselves to things of cultural importance," I said. "You ought to go, too, Mark, and you, Fuzzy."

"Count me out," said Fuzzy, displaying a strength of character I had not hitherto suspected. "Nebraska is playing Miami tonight."

After lunch, Mark and I walked to algebra together. "I thought you told me classical music bored you," he said. "I'm sure you did. What's going on?"

"Don't you see that Bix is just going to that concert in order to make up to Celia?"

"I know why Bix is going, all right. What I don't get is why you think we should go."

"I think we ought to stand by in case Bix needs us."

"Oh, for Pete's sake."

"I'm serious, Mark. Don't you see? Bix isn't like you and me. We are reasonable, thinking people. We consider the consequences. Bix is like a tidal wave. He doesn't think, he doesn't ask himself what is going to happen next, he just goes ahead and does things. Look at the fixes he gets himself in! And I promised Chris I'd help look out for him."

"Is that all it is? That you promised Chris?"

"Well, of course, now that I've gotten to know Bix, I want to help out even more."

"Right."

"You don't sound very happy. Are you going to go with me or not?"

"You're out of your mind, but I guess you need a ride over there."

"I sure don't want to ride with Bix, if that's what you mean."

"Okay. I'll drive you."

I looked up at him, fighting off the impulse to give him a big hug. Mark was absolutely my favorite friendly giant.

"Mark," I said, suddenly, "do you miss Chris a lot?"

He paused a minute to think about it. "Well, it's just that the gang is different since she's gone, you know? It's a different mix, the flavor is different, somehow. I can't quite put my finger on it."

I had been hoping he would say, "Oh, you're just as good as Chris, Katy. It doesn't matter that you don't know how to drive or ski or play pinochle." So much for my luck in fishing for compliments.

"It's that you're a girl," he said, as if pleased that he had finally defined the problem. "That's what it is."

"But Chris is a girl, too," I pointed out quite reasonably.

"That's different," he said.

The bell near me went off like a bomb and I broke into a run. Late to algebra again.

Algebra is a subject from which my attention wanders in the best of circumstances. And with so much on my mind—how to keep Bix from fighting, how to make Celia fall for Bix, and how to figure out what Mark was getting at when he made that crack about me being a girl—I found myself gazing vacantly out the window. From the second story window of Mr. Hatchard's class, I had a good view of the flagpole and the semicircular drive in front of the school, but the scene didn't seem particularly interesting until I saw Peyton walking across the grass heading in the direction of the parking lot. He was carrying his books and he glanced up in my direction, his mirrored sunglasses flashing in the sun. I drew away from the window. Even though I knew he couldn't see me, there was something malevolent about the way he looked at the school building that made me want to duck in case he threw a bomb in my direction.

"Maybe I'd better put that equation on the board for you," Mr. Hatchard was telling the class.

I forced my eyes in the direction of the board because I needed all the help I could get in algebra. But I kept thinking—why was Peyton leaving school early? He didn't look sick. I wished I hadn't heard those threats he was making near the water fountain.

After school Mark and Fuzzy and I all went over to Bix's house. Bix's mother had made a double batch of brownies before she had left for the women's circle meeting. Mrs. Bixby, I learned, was always trying subtle ploys to keep Bix at home so he wouldn't go out cruising. Unfortunately, she would need more than subtle ploys to do that. In fact, probably the only ploy that would work would be the not-so-subtle one of draining his gas tank.

Mark crowned his brownies with a dollop of vanilla ice cream then joined the rest of us, who were draped over the wicker furniture on Bix's screened front porch.

"Fancy stereo setup," Mark commented as he let himself down into a basket-shaped chair. "Where'd it come from?"

He was looking at the table in the corner that contained a pool cue and a few pool balls, an old bingo set, a tennis racket in need of restringing and a stack of moth-eaten *National Geographics* in addition to a lot of stereo components.

Bix glanced up at the table. "Dunno," he said. He returned his attention to the jacket of a record he was holding. "Okay, how's this—and then I say,'I happened to notice that the polyphonic element is related to the Fugue in G Minor.' "

"Sounds hard to remember," commented Fuzzy. "And what if she catches on that it came off a record jacket?"

"Wait a minute," I said. "Stop everything!"

"You think it's a bad idea, too, huh?" said Bix, downcast.

"No, no, not that. What do you *mean* you don't know where the stereo came from?"

"Never saw it before," said Bix, shrugging.

I got up and went over to look at the speakers. "But it looks practically brand-new." I ran my fingers across the bingo game and the tennis racket and noticed that the stereo was the only thing on the table that didn't have a coat of dust on it. "Do you think your parents just bought it?" I asked.

"Not hardly," said Bix. "We've started this new strict budget where Mom's rationing the toothpaste."

Mark joined me over at the table. "It looks like a pretty expensive setup to me," he said. "And as Katy says, it looks brand-new. I can't see somebody giving it away. Are you sure your parents didn't buy it?"

"You got to be kidding. You know how my dad is always begging for a little peace and quiet around here. Actually, he hates music. Says it interrupts his thoughts."

"I have a bad feeling about this," I said. "I think we'd better hide all these components. Let's put them in the trunk of Mark's car, okay? Here, come on everybody, let's move it. Mark, you take the turntable, it's the heaviest. Come on, grab a component and move as fast as you can."

"What's going on?" asked Bix. "Hey, what are you doing?"

I was already hoisting the receiver onto one hip. "I think maybe Peyton planted these here. He's out to get you, Bix."

"What gives you that idea?" asked Bix.

"Don't argue!" I said. "Move!"

Fuzzy looked at me suspiciously. "I think you're going crackers, Katy. You've probably been studying too hard."

"Humor me," I snapped, staggering out the screened door with the receiver.

"Come on, you guys," said Mark, "grab a component and come on. It's easy enough to move it all back if Katy's wrong."

With all of us working on it, it only took a few minutes to get everything out to Mark's car and lock the trunk. "The only thing is," I said, suddenly uncertain, "I'm not sure the police need a warrant to search a car. Well, it's past praying for now. Let's get back to the front porch. And be sure to look innocent."

"But we are innocent," Fuzzy bleated.

A minute later we were back on the screened porch, a little breathless. Mark was checking out his ice cream—now thoroughly melted—with his face contorted into an expression of disgust. Then the police car drove up.

I could not resist shooting a triumphant look at Fuzzy.

A couple of officers in uniform got out and approached the house. They paused when they got as far as Bix's car, parked in the driveway. I could see them circling it disapprovingly. I suppose they didn't care for the modifications he had made to it. But to my relief, they showed no interest at all in Mark's car, where the stereo was hidden.

They looked huge and intimidating standing on the front stoop. They were like enormous shadows blocking the light. When they knocked on the screen door, the whole door shivered as if it were having awful premonitions. Bix got up and pulled it open.

"Are you Bix Bixby?" one of them asked.

"Yes, sir," said Bix. "Is anything wrong?"

The officer didn't reply at first. Both policemen were wearing mirrored sunglasses and blue uniforms fetchingly accessorized with matching guns in holsters. They had large jaws and their faces were as expressionless as tombstones. Slowly they turned their heads, looking around the front porch, their jaws working. Then, one of them said, "Mind if we look around?"

"My parents aren't at home right now," Bix said, "but I guess that would be all right. What are you looking for?"

I thought Bix was doing very well at looking all alarmed innocence. Of course, he was innocent and he was alarmed, but I knew from personal experience that it is quite possible to be innocent and yet to look like a skulking convict. I had the feeling I was looking like one that very minute.

The police officers didn't answer Bix's question but stepped into the porch and began looking around. They even stooped down and peered under the basket chair Mark was sprawled on. I had a moment of panic when I remembered that we hadn't checked inside the house. What if Peyton had stashed more loot in there? Then I recalled watching Bix unlock the house when we got in from school. His parents probably always kept the place locked. That was undoubtedly why the stereo had been left on the front porch to begin with.

Bix went inside with the police. They were in there for some time while Mark and Fuzzy and I looked at one another with wide eyes, afraid to say a word. Finally, they came out.

"My parents are really going to want to know what this is about, officer," said Bix.

"You know Bix's father, the Reverend George Bixby?" I put in.

For the first time, the policemen began to look a little uncertain. One of them frowned and looked at his clipboard. "We've had a report from Peyton

Richardson, Jr. of stolen property. He says he saw you hanging around his house yesterday when he went out and that when he came back, his entire stereo system was missing."

"Hanging around his house?" said Bix. "I haven't even been near his house!" Bix glanced at me. "He must have me mixed up with somebody else."

"Bix and Peyton got in a fight the other day at school and Peyton lost," I put in. "Maybe Peyton just wants to think it was Bix who took his stereo."

The police did not comment on that. One of them intoned, "Larceny is a serious offense."

We listened to that in respectful silence.

Finally, to our immense relief, they left.

"Golly," I said, watching them move toward their car. "Talk about ominous looking. You know those Fates they have in the Latin book? They ought to dress them in blue uniforms and give them leather belts. Super creepy."

"Don't let them hear you," muttered Mark.

"They can't hear me," I said. But after that we all sat stiffly, in silence, until they had driven away.

Then we all started talking at once.

"Told you so!"

"Where does Peyton get off—"

"Good grief, what a close shave!"

"How did you know, Katy? What made you suspect—"

"Well," I said, when the furor began to subside, "I've been worried ever since I heard Peyton breathing threats at the water fountain this morning. He kept saying Bix was going to be sorry. I had a feeling he might try something."

"I wish you hadn't mentioned that fight to the police," said Bix uneasily. "I'd hate for it to get back to my father."

"Good grief, Bix," Mark said, "a couple hundred people saw you slug him."

"I thought I'd better tell the police about the fight," I said. "I needed to let the police know he had a grudge against you. Otherwise, what's to stop him from finding out tomorrow that his television is missing or his savings bonds or the gold fillings in his teeth?"

"I'd like to show that Peyton a thing or two," growled Bix, drawing his hand into a fist.

Mark said, "Forget it, Bix. Hitting him won't work."

Bix slumped back in his chair and laughed. "I know it. Jeez, even I know it. But what are we going to do?"

"Maybe nothing," said Mark. "For all we know, he's already having second thoughts. Framing somebody for a larceny rap is a serious step. He's probably already wishing he didn't do it."

Bix and I gave each other a meaningful look. An easygoing sort like Mark might figure Peyton was cooling down, but Bix and I weren't counting on it.

"I doubt if he'll try this again," Mark went on.

"Yeah," I said. "Next time he'll try something different."

* * *

It was a sobered bunch who showed up that evening for the celebration of Mozart in the large choir room of First Presbyterian Church. I wore my blue silk dress with Mom's pearls, and Bix and Mark were just barely recognizable dressed in their good dark suits.

The audience assembled for Mozart seemed to be mostly a thin and earnest bunch. I counted fifteen strands of pearls and there was a complete and total absence of raucous laughter.

Mark fingered his program uneasily. "What did you mean this afternoon when you said Peyton was going to try something else," he muttered.

"He's been humiliated. Can't you tell that Peyton thinks he's one of the aristocrats of Hampstead High? The green jacket club, the way those guys stand—it all fits. He can't take being beaten by Bix because it's a blow to his image as someone who's above all the rest of us. He's got to get revenge to restore his status in his own eyes. The first try didn't work out, so he'll try again."

"You sound awfully sure. Is that woman's intuition?"

"That's rational deduction. Elementary, my dear Mark."

"Will you two cut it out? They're going to start," said Bix. He was looking intently at the line of performers who were now filing out to stand in front of their flute stands.

"What am I going to do with the blinking stereo in the trunk of my car?" grumbled Mark. "That's what I want to know."

"Just don't try to sell it to a fence," I advised.

When the piercing notes of flute music split the air, Bix shot us a threatening look, so I folded my hands and tried to listen. It was not easy. I must have been frightened by a tuba in my infancy or something because I just can't seem to keep my mind on music unless I can sing it. After about four beats of unadorned music my mind is off gathering nasturtiums. Tonight it was no different. Four beats and my mind had left Mozart altogether and was busy trying to figure out what Peyton was going to be up to next. It was tough trying to put myself into his devious little mind, but the more I thought about it the more I thought that his second move would probably be pretty similar to his first. Just as habitual criminals have their telltale MO, or method of operation, so I was sure Peyton would use roughly the same method the second time as the first. He would not be likely, for example, to move from framing Bix to a completely different approach such as setting a tiger pit trap full of sharpened stakes. Still, I couldn't see how he could report more stolen items to the police. They were bound to get suspicious of him. Particularly after what I had told them about there being bad blood between him and Bix.

Next to me Bix was freezing like a bird dog, so I realized that Celia was playing a solo passage and I tried to pay attention. I couldn't figure out exactly where we were on the program, but I could tell that Celia's flute had a very full strong tone, unlike some of the others that sounded kind of reedy, and she didn't seem to miss any notes. That was about as far as my music appreciation went. But I knew she wouldn't have been chosen for the solo part over all those grown women unless she'd been pretty good. And I had to admit, she did look like an angel up there with her blond hair falling past her shoulders and her rings catching the light as her long, tapered fingers played on the keys. Bix, naturally, was totally entranced. He was so still, I had to struggle with the impulse to give him mouth-to-mouth resuscitation. He definitely had a bad case. There was no doubt about that.

At last Mozart had been thoroughly saluted, and after a prolonged bout of well-bred applause we dispersed to the reception to congratulate the artists.

"Hey, I didn't realize they had food at these things," said Mark, cheering up as he moved like a magnet toward the table full of home-baked cookies.

Bix swallowed hard and made his way over to Celia. I happened to be standing behind a nearby palm tree and saw the entire thing.

"That was beautiful, Celia. I mean, you really do play awfully well," he said.

"Thank you," she said in a strange voice. It was not her normal voice at all, it was strictly the sort of voice in which the ice goddess deigns to speak to the troll. At once she turned away and began talking to an elderly man who was leaning feebly on a walker.

Bix looked over at me helplessly.

I stepped out from behind the palm and began to guide him in the direction of the refreshments table. "Try the chocolate pinwheels," I suggested. "And Mark seems to think the brownies are especially good. I see three on his plate."

"What did I do?" he asked me in an agonized whisper. "She acts as if I'd killed somebody. I'm going to go over there and make her tell me what's the matter."

"Oh, no, you're not," I said. I raised a finger to signal Mark. When he reached me I muttered, "We'd better get Bix out of here. If we stay much longer he's going to be challenging that old man with the walker to a duel."

Mark nodded, put one last piece of fudge in his pocket, and together we hurried Bix out to the parking lot.

"Why can't I make her tell me what's going on?" Bix burst out when we got outside.

"Because if you cause a scene at the reception you'll embarrass her in front of all her flute-playing friends and she'll never speak to you again, that's why," I said.

This silenced Bix, but he looked perfectly awful. His skin seemed to be stretched more tightly over the delicately chiseled bones of his face, and under the dim parking lot lights his eyes looked dark.

"Don't worry," I said. "I'm supposed to study chemistry with her tomorrow night and I'll very tactfully bring the subject around to what it is she is angry about and then I'll try to bring her around to see your point of view."

Bix breathed deeply. "You're a real friend, Katy. Call me up as soon as you talk to her, okay?"

I only hoped it was something I was going to be able to put right because unless I missed my guess, Celia had heard about the epic fight.

Chapter Five

The next evening, I showed up at Celia's house with my chemistry notes under my arm. She met me at the door and led me back to her room. "I heard you at the flute concert last night," I said. "You really did a nice job."

"Thank you," she said. She didn't seem very interested in discussing her performance, which was just as well since that exhausted my supply of intelligent comments.

I sat down, took out my notes and spread them out on her bed. "Do you think we should start by comparing our notes or would you rather ask each other questions?" I asked.

"I noticed that you were there last night," she said, biting on her lip.

This is better than I hoped for, I thought. She is actually trying to work around to talking about Bix. I won't even need to figure out a way to bring it up.

"Did you go with Bix?" she said carelessly, shuffling through her own notes.

"Actually, I got a ride with Mark but then we all sat together. What was going on between you and Bix? Why were you so nasty to him after the concert?"

"He's just impossible, that's all!" she exploded. "Did you see poor Peyton?"

"Yeah." I grinned. "He looked like a raccoon, didn't he?"

"You think that's funny? That Bix jumped on him and beat him unmercifully for no good reason? I think it's horrible. He knew Peyton couldn't defend himself. Peyton is too sensitive to be a fighter."

"He certainly has a glass jaw," I recalled with satisfaction.

"I'm surprised at you, Katy. I thought you were a civilized human being. Obviously, I was wrong."

"Now wait a minute. I think Bix was out of line to hit Peyton, but you have to keep in mind that he had a lot of provocation."

"Nothing can justify people behaving like animals," said Celia.

"Maybe not, but it's only fair to remember that Peyton hit Bix first. At least, he tried to hit him," I amended, "but Bix ducked. And second, the only reason they got in the fight was because Bix heard

Peyton making some insulting remarks when you went by.''

"That's what Bix told you."

"Well, Bix may have a hot temper, but I don't think anybody would say he was a liar."

"He probably misinterpreted what Peyton said. Bix is so quick to fly off the handle," she said, turning her shapely nose up in the air.

I was more amused than anything else. One thing I could see was that Celia really wanted to talk about Bix. She had said she was afraid of being distracted from her work by a boy, but the truth was, she was already distracted. I had been ready to study for the chemistry test. It was Celia who wanted to spend the whole night talking about Bix's shortcomings. My guess was that meant that Bix already had the battle half won, even though Celia didn't seem to know it yet.

I reached for my chemistry book. "There were a couple of hundred witnesses to Peyton throwing the first punch. Ask anybody."

"I wish I'd been there," said Celia. When I looked at her in surprise, she added hastily, "So I could see for myself what happened, of course."

"Naturally," I said. "I have to say, I think you really hurt Bix when you snubbed him at the reception." I added cunningly, "He's very sensitive, you know."

"Bix? Sensitive? Ha!" she said. She folded her arms across her chest.

"Just because Bix doesn't go around crying on people's shoulders doesn't mean he doesn't have feelings, too. He was very deeply hurt, you can take it from me. He looked awful afterward out in the parking lot. Think about it—here is this girl he admires, he politely compliments her on her playing and she practically slaps his face."

"I thought he had beaten up poor Peyton."

"You were wrong. Peyton must have got those black eyes when he hit the ground because except for a little clip on the ear, Bix only hit him once. I think it would be nice if you would apologize to Bix, that's what I think. I'm not saying Bix is perfect, but there's no call to treat him like a murderer."

Her chemistry book slipped out of her fingers and as she groped for it on the floor I saw that her eyes were filling up with tears. "Oh, I don't know what to do, Katy," she said. "I see exactly what you're saying. I mean, I can see that I got the wrong idea about that fight and I just feel awful that I was so nasty. It's not like me. I don't know what got into me."

"So just apologize. You'll feel heaps better."

"You don't understand. I'm afraid if I apologize, Bix will start telling me how he loves me and everything," she sniffled. She was getting rather red in the face. "I like him, but why does he have to come on so strong? It's...it's...I don't like it," she finished lamely.

"Moderation isn't Bix's strong point," I admitted reluctantly.

"I just want to be friends. Why can't we be friends?"

I had the feeling that was a very old question, and I certainly didn't have the answer to it.

"Why don't you just apologize and then you'll know that at least you did the right thing."

"That's true," she said, brightening. "Of course, it was wrong, definitely wrong for Bix to get into that fight, but after all, I can't expect other people to live by my principles. That would be very narrow-minded of me. I'll just make a simple apology and then I'll say that I hope we can go on being friends."

"Sounds good," I said.

Now, I thought, all I have to do is to persuade Bix not to fling his heart at Celia's feet at a stage of the relationship where her likely reaction would be, "Is this your heart? Oh, yuck!" Being an adviser on romantic matters was turning out to be a very demanding job.

The next day was a big day for me. I successfully parallel parked. Bix had been taking me out every afternoon for an intensive driving lesson, and while I came very far from meeting his standards, he did allow as how he thought I was ready to pass the test.

"I'll never forget the way you helped me out with this junk with Celia," he said awkwardly as we were driving back to my place.

"When I pass my driver's test, we'll call it even," I said. "But remember what I said. Keep it light. Keep it friendly. Don't push her. If you ask my personal opinion, I have to say I think the girl is sold on you already, but she does not like being crowded."

"Is it crowding somebody to let her know you care about her?" Bix asked from between clenched teeth.

"Yes," I said bluntly. "Now remember. Okay?"

He managed a weak smile as he let me off in front of my house. I skipped up the front walk and flung the door open. "Mom!" I called. "I'm ready to take my driver's test!"

Mom came to the door of the kitchen wiping her hands on her apron. "What did you say, Katy? I thought I heard something about a driver's test."

"Bix thinks I'm ready. I parallel parked today."

"Bix has been giving you driving lessons?"

"Well, yes."

"I thought you said you were going to the library."

Actually, I had cleverly given that impression by explaining the first time that we were going to the library to study. After that I just said, "Bye, Mom, we're off," when we left and let her draw her own conclusions.

"Why would we be going to the library every single day?" I asked.

"I guess I thought you were interested in Bix," smiled Mom. "I thought you were murmuring sweet nothings over the reference books."

"Bix and me? You must be kidding. When can you take me for the driving test, huh?"

"I still don't understand how Bix taught you to drive. Aren't you supposed to have someone older than eighteen with you in the car when you only have a learner's permit?''

''We were out on these back roads on his uncle's farm and I don't think the laws apply there, Mom,'' I said, heading rapidly back to my room to avoid further probing questions. ''Could you take me this afternoon? It's really important for me to have my license. At Hampstead, only outcasts don't have their licenses.'' I paused when I thought of a parting shot. ''And if I had my license I could take Caroline to her ballet lessons and her piano lessons.''

Perhaps spurred by the idea that I could help with the chauffeuring of Caroline, Mom took me to get my license that very afternoon. I passed the test on the first try. The examiner complimented Mom on my parallel parking and she nearly passed out from surprise. I guess the memory of the pleated fender of Mr. Burney's new Plymouth was still fresh in her mind.

When they handed me my license, I felt so grown up I couldn't stand it. Even though I had my driver's license, I intended to go on riding to school with Mark if I could. Since I had gotten used to riding with him, it seemed to me that it would be lonely to ride to school all by myself. Also, I just liked to be around Mark. Of course, I saw plenty of him when I was hanging around with the guys but that wasn't the same.

When I climbed into the blue Studebaker the next morning, I proudly displayed my license to him. He held up one hand as if he were blinded by the glory of it. "Like wild, Katy. They're letting you loose on the roads unattended," he said.

"That's right," I said, tucking it back in my wallet. "But would it be okay if I still ride to school with you?"

"Sure."

"I'd be happy to chip in on the gas."

"Don't worry about it."

"You see, sometimes Mom needs the car during the day. I don't like to take it all day."

"It's fine. You're right on my way."

I did not mention anything to Mark about how I enjoyed his company because I was following my own romantic advice and was anxious not to crowd him. Actually, I had begun to have hopes for a warm and beautiful relationship between me and Mark, but I hadn't quite figured out the details, like how to get him to see it my way.

He turned onto the broad avenue. "You got the license just in time. Things are heating up around here. Halloween's coming. Big day. People will be going out and getting their costumes—pointy teeth, fake blood, gore, repulsive green skin, slimy bloodshot eyes, everything you need for a fun time. Since I'm on the committee for the Halloween bash, a combination carnival and dance, which we earnestly hope will show an increase in attendance over last year's lackluster pumpkin festival, I took the liberty of suggesting you as the gypsy for the fortune teller's tent."

I looked at him approvingly. "What a terrific idea! I will be a total smash at the fortune teller's tent with my acute knowledge of the workings of the human mind, my insight."

"Your modesty," he added.

"That too. Oh, I can't wait. Who are you going as?"

"I'm thinking of Mark Antony," he said. "I figure I can manage that with a sheet and a laurel wreath."

"Why not Julius Caesar?" I asked.

"Julius Caesar was thin. Also, he was balding. Whereas Antony, as far as I know, had a full head of hair and I kind of think he went to seed toward the end. You know, too much wine, women and song, the world well lost for love and all that."

"Oh, you haven't gone to seed," I said, punching him lightly. "But have you thought of this? Will it be any fun when people will be able to recognize you? A sheet and a laurel wreath aren't exactly a disguise."

"There isn't much point in a disguise when you're as big as I am."

He had me there. I had to admit that very few people in the school were as tall and practically no one was as all around big as Mark.

"Well, in that case, I think you'd make a terrific Mark Antony. I'd be Cleopatra for you, except that I'm sure I'd make a much better gypsy. I can see it now, the mysterious east, the crystal ball. Do you think I should have a black cat?"

"That's witches you're thinking of. They're the ones with the black cats."

"I guess so. And besides if I had a black cat Peyton wouldn't come near me, as superstitious as he is, and I'm dying to read him a creepy fortune."

"An excellent idea. Speaking of creepy, my little sister tells me she is going to be Dracula," said Mark. "She'll be the only girl Dracula in the third grade."

"I didn't know your little sister was in the third grade. Does she know my sister, Caroline?"

"They are the closest of friends. I believe that means they hate each other on alternate weeks and spend the rest of the time happily gossiping about the other girls."

"Isn't that funny. I didn't know that. Caroline never talks to me anymore."

"Maybe you're never at home anymore."

I was forced to admit there might be some truth in that. I had been hot in pursuit of my driver's license for some weeks.

"I don't think it's just that, Mark. You're easy to talk to."

"Yep, good old, easy-to-talk-to Mark," he said bitterly.

I frowned a little. He seemed to be in a strange kind of mood. I had never thought before that Mark was at all moody. It just went to show that no matter how well you thought you knew people, there were always surprises.

I had been about to tell him about my talk with Celia, but I decided to hold off until he was more like his old self. In fact, it might be better not to mention it at all. When I thought about it, I was not absolutely sure that Bix wanted everybody to get a play-by-play account of his relationship with Celia. It was a delicate personal matter, after all. I was sure I wouldn't want my friends keeping score on the progress of my romance.

Mark was right about the interest in Halloween starting to peek. As nearly as I could make out, during homeroom, a full scale panic was in progress among those who had planned to be monsters on account of a severe local shortage of slime. Mrs. Fergusson finally gave up trying to read the day's announcements and the period degenerated into a babble of technical talk about gum adhesive, greasepaint and wigs. I heard Bobby Hinson saying that plenty of gorilla suits were available, but he was worried the night might be too warm to be a gorilla even if he didn't wear a thing under the suit. Esmée Parkinson agreed that one couldn't be too careful in choosing one's costume. Last year she had gone as a Christmas package and in the big boxy costume she hadn't been able to sit down all night. Billy Tyler seemed to be trying to persuade four guys to spend the evening as horses so he could make a grand entrance as a Roman charioteer. I should have guessed that Halloween was exactly the kind of holiday that Hampstead High would choose to take to its heart.

After class, Phoebe Hatch, a serious-looking girl I hadn't noticed much before, came up to me holding a small spiral bound notebook. "Mark says you can do the fortune teller's tent," she said, jotting my name down in her book. "We're using Tony Alvarez's little brother's tent so you may want to do some work covering up the Indian Bob insignia on the side. Mrs. Wiggins is supplying the crystal ball. I'm providing the small round table. Do you have a tablecloth we can use?"

I nodded. Amid the general excitement, I felt proud to be doing my humble bit at the fortune teller's tent.

Phoebe shot me a calculating glance. "Where do you know Mark from? I don't remember seeing you around here before."

"We were introduced by a mutual friend," I said sweetly. I was wondering where *she* knew Mark from, and I was also wondering what exactly her intentions were.

"What are you going to be for Halloween?" I asked, looking her up and down critically.

She smiled. "I'm going as Mata Hari."

I did not find that reassuring.

When I got in from school that afternoon, I gave some thought to what Mark said. Maybe I hadn't been spending enough time at home just lately. Maybe I should engage Caroline in a little conversation, find out how things were going with her at school, have a heart-to-heart talk with my little sister.

I found her in front of the full-length mirror in the hall. She was fastening on a necklace made of pink plastic beads. It boasted a large pink pendant with the legend Sweety Pie written on it in gold. This put the finishing touch to an ensemble consisting of pink jogging shoes, red and green striped stockings, a short pink skirt and layers of green and pink cotton jackets. I could never decide whether Caroline was trying to look like a punk rocker or a fruit cocktail.

I pulled up a chair and smiled at her. "Hi, there, Caro," I said. "What's up?"

She looked at me suspiciously, then opened her mouth wide and yelled, "Ma-ma! Katy's bothering me!"

"I'm not bothering you! I just wanted to say hello, find out how school is going and all. Say, what are you going to be for Halloween?"

She looked at me suspiciously. "A witch," she said.

It figured.

I decided it was better to try to work on developing a relationship with Caroline in small doses. Maybe I would be able to win her confidence bit by bit while chauffeuring her around for her various lessons.

A more manageable project right now, perhaps, would be my Halloween costume. As a fortune teller I would need to look completely different from my usual self. I would have little credibility if people could see that the fortune teller was just Katy Callahan from their fifth period Algebra class.

I decided to go to the fabric store and stock up on remnants to make a gypsy-type flounced skirt and blouse. After my visit to the fabric shop, a quick dash to the corner drug store provided me with Dark Rachel makeup base, Ruby Lips lipstick and a pair of brassy jangling earrings that were absolutely perfect. They looked like small bird cages that had been mugged and forced to drop their pocket change. I held them up to the light, shook them a little and watched the little copper coins jiggling under the cages. Ideal. Now all I needed was a hair piece. I sensed that gypsies did not have short, fluffy hair like mine. A brief stop at Flip Your Wig supplied a full, long swatch of hair that could be attached to my own with combs. With a couple of roses stuck in all that hair, I should look sufficiently gypsyish.

It took me several evenings of hard work to make my costume, but it was worth it because by the time I had finished sewing all those rows and rows of taffeta ruffles in orange and green—the only colors that had been available on the remnant table, the effect was nothing if not colorful.

Chapter Six

Halloween night, the air in the fortune teller's tent was more than a little bit stuffy. I was just as glad Mrs. Wiggins had, for safety reasons, overruled the idea of having a candle on my little table. It would have only burned up oxygen and I didn't need the light. The rafters of the gym had been hung with colored bulbs and enough of the light shone through the fabric of the tent to give my crystal ball the necessary faint mysterious glow.

I could hear the band playing at the other end of the gym, and splashing and giggling sounds were coming from the apple bob tubs over near the basketball hoops. Dark shadows played against the walls of my tent as couples danced close by outside.

The flap of the tent opened and Mark squeezed his way inside. "Brought you some punch," he said, sliding a cup across the table past my crystal ball. He eyed the low canvas roof of the tent and tugged uncomfortably at the shoulder of his toga. "Lucky thing you don't have claustrophobia," he said.

"Business has been great," I said. "It's slacking off now that the music has started, but I've been really busy. Everybody wants to know the future."

"What do you tell them?"

"Mostly I say some good, some bad. That's a safe bet. Then I throw in the odd tall stranger and the unexpected good fortune without which no fortune is complete. Then, and this is where I draw on psychology, I tell them that they really want some one thing to happen, but there is just one thing standing in their way."

"Is that a safe bet, too?"

"Sure," I said. "Nobody's ever happy with what they've got. You didn't happen to bring me anything to eat, did you?"

He fished a couple of cookies and a brownie out of the pocket of his toga and handed them over.

"There's one unexpected fringe benefit," I said, biting into the brownie. "I get to overhear all these weird conversations. People come right up outside of the tent and talk as if I'm not here."

"The tent is like a duck blind," Mark commented.

"I guess. Of course, I suppose the ethical thing would be for me to keep clearing my throat all evening."

"But you don't."

"Well, my throat's been getting a little dry until you so sweetly showed up with the punch."

"So do I get my fortune told by the gypsy?"

"Naturally." I waved my hands over the crystal ball and halfway closed my eyes, then began speaking in my throaty gypsy voice. "I see a wonderful girl in your future," I said. "She is very charming and intelligent and she is crazy about you. Yes, I see here a something, a something I cannot quite make it out. Something surprising. Perhaps there is a danger, I cannot be sure."

Mark was bending anxiously over the crystal ball. "What else?" he said.

I giggled. "See what I mean?" I said. "People want to believe this stuff. It's a piece of cake."

He straightened up, self-consciously rearranging the gathered shoulder of his toga. "Any sign of Peyton yet?"

"Not yet. But if he's here tonight at all, I'm betting he can't pass up the gypsy's tent."

"Oh, he's here, all right. He's one of the three Musketeers with the big hat and feather, doublet and everything. They must have got the setups from some costume place in Raleigh. I better shove off. I don't want to scare him away."

"Come back later and I'll fill you in on how it went."

When Mark backed out of the tent flap it looked for a minute as if he might take the tent with him, but when it sort of shuddered all over, he scrunched down even lower and managed to clear it. Indian Bob's kiddie tent had not been made for people of Mark's dimensions.

After he left, a pair of giggling sophomore girls insisted on coming in together, which was a really tight squeeze. When I predicted that one of them would make a killing on the stock market and the other had a destiny of travel and romance, they broke into hysterical giggles and the tent jiggled so much I was alarmed. I only hoped Peyton would show up before the whole thing collapsed.

After the girls left, I heard Mrs. Wiggins's voice behind me, which caused me to jump, but then I realized she was outside the tent.

"I don't know, Harvey," she was saying. "I think the rice paddy idea has a lot to recommend it."

The raspy voice that answered her, I recognized as the coach. He sounded very depressed. "That's all I need," he was saying. "It's not enough that I've got a team with a 0-6 season, I've got to be the only coach in the conference that's got his own student body trying to turn his football field into a rice paddy. Do I have to tell you what this does to the morale of the players, not to know week to week whether they're going to be splashing around out there like ducks?"

His voice grew fainter as they moved away and suddenly the flap of the tent opened and Peyton came in. To get inside, he had to take off his big hat, which had a curled-up brim and a huge sweeping ostrich feather. He laid it on the floor and leaned toward me. I involuntarily drew away from him. He had terrible breath, as if he were exhaling lighter fluid. Then I noticed that his fake moustache was on crooked and his face was flushed. In a flash of brilliant deduction, it hit me that he must have been drinking.

"You tell fortunes?" he asked, wobbling precariously on the stool.

"Yas," I said in my low gypsy voice. "The gypsy, she tells the fortunes. She sees into the future. She sees into your mind."

He looked uncomfortable after that, but still interested. He bent down and tried to peer directly into the crystal ball.

I shielded it with my hands. "Do not get the fingerprints on the crystal ball, if you please."

"Oh, right, sorry," he said.

But then an odd thing happened. I realized I couldn't tell Peyton the awful fortune I had made up about how his crimes would find him out and his fingernails would fall off and his green jacket would get sloshed with indelible ink. The problem was he was such a sucker for the fortune telling that he would have believed it. I just couldn't take advantage of him that way. It didn't seem fair.

With a thudding sense of disappointment, I mentally shelved my specially designed Peyton fortune and instead began the standard spiel. "The future will bring good things and it will bring bad things."

He licked his lips. "Sort of a mixed bag, huh?"

"Pre-cisely. I see, I cannot quite make it out now, yes, I see some sort of difficulty, it may be a danger, I cannot say."

"What about girls?" said Peyton.

"The ball is very cloudy. I cannot say. You will be taking a journey."

"That must be to New York," he said. "We're going to go up there and see some shows."

"Possibly that it is. I cannot tell. A journey. I see strange shapes, colors, confusion. Much is going on. Much confusion."

Peyton looked around him anxiously, then bent forward and whispered to me. "Tell me this. You don't see anybody getting beat up in there, do you?"

This was a toughy. I decided to hedge a little. "I see nobody being beat up without a good reason," I said finally.

There was a long silence as, with his mouth open, he stared at the crystal ball. "Is that all?"

"That is all. The crystal ball has spoken."

"Oh," he said.

He picked up his hat and backed unsteadily out of the tent. After he left, I sat there a second feeling stupid. I had had a golden opportunity and I had blown it. I should have really scared him, but I had missed my chance. What was I going to tell Mark when he came back to see how it had gone?

"Bix," Celia's voice called behind me.

"Celia!" said Bix. He couldn't have sounded closer if he'd been sitting on the crystal ball. They must have been standing right outside the tent.

"I just want to apologize for the way I acted at the Mozart festival," Celia said unsteadily. "I feel terrible about it. I can't tell you how bad I feel."

"Celia!" said Bix, in a perfectly idiotic voice.

I realized, with horror, that it was too late for me to clear my throat. Things had already gotten too embarrassing for that. I would just have to sit here and cover my ears.

I did cover my ears, but unfortunately, I could hear what was going on anyway.

"Let go of my hands!" said Celia in her ice goddess voice.

"Let's not fight," said Bix. "I can't stand it when you get mad at me. You know how I feel about you."

"Let go of my hands or I will scream," said Celia, sounding very determined.

"Scream! Good grief, what have I ever done except get—get fond of you," said Bix, apparently remembering my advice too late.

"If you will just please go away and leave me alone, I would appreciate it," said Celia.

"Aaaagh," said Bix. I heard no more from him so I presumed he had stomped away.

I covered my face with my hands as I heard Celia sniffling outside.

"What's wrong?" said Peyton's voice. My eyes flew open in alarm.

"Oh, Peyton," Celia said. "I have such a terrible headache, all of a sudden. I . . . I get these awful headaches. I mean, it looks as if I'm crying, but it's just that I really need an aspirin or something, I guess."

"I'll take you home."

"But I came with Susannah and Cissy and Alan."

"Well, you don't want to take them away from the party, do you?"

"But are you ready to go home?"

"I'm pretty tired," said Peyton, "to tell you the truth." This was convincing enough since he sounded a little woozy.

Their voices were growing dimmer and I suddenly realized that Celia was actually leaving with Peyton, Peyton who was not only stewed to the gills but who was just looking for a chance to get back at Dix. I was sure that if Celia hadn't been so upset, she would have noticed herself that it wasn't such a good idea. What if Peyton wrecked the car? Or what if he tried to take her somewhere she didn't want to go, like out to the lake instead of home?

I jumped up and banged my head on the ridgepole of the tent causing the whole tent to shudder like Jell-O. Luckily, it did not collapse on me. I got my purse from under the table, pulled a piece of paper out of it, and scrawled, "The gypsy is away on sabbatical." I stuck it to the flap of the tent with a bobby pin. Then, my flounces rustling as I ran, I headed out the back door of the gym toward the parking lot. I was not sure exactly what I was going to do, but I thought it was best to keep Peyton and Celia in my sight. I could always decide what to do later.

I had stepped out the gym door and was casting my eyes around the parking lot when suddenly Bix appeared at my side. "What's the matter?" he asked.

"Celia's left with Peyton," I said. "And he's been drinking."

Bix made an inarticulate strangled sound deep in his throat. Suddenly I spotted Mom's car nearby. In the heat of the moment, I couldn't remember where I had parked, so I figured it was lucky I happened to spot the car so close by. I dashed over and jumped in. Bix was in the other side of the seat before I had even closed my door.

I stuck my key in the ignition. The key went in smoothly enough but for some reason it wouldn't turn.

"This is a heck of a time for you to forget how to start the car," Bix growled.

"It's not that. The key must be warped or something." I kept trying to twist it, but suddenly Bix reached over me, released the hood latch and then jumped out of the car.

"What are you doing?"

"Hot wiring it," came the voice from under the hood. I saw the glint of metal under the hood and then to my amazement the engine leaped into life. Bix slammed the hood shut and jumped back in the car. "Drive," he said.

I drove the car out of the lot. "How did you do that?" I asked.

"Screwdriver attachment on my pocketknife," he said. "You just get a spark to jump between the points. Which way did they go?"

I drove out on the street in front of the school and then turned west. "He said he was going to take her home, so he'd have to start out in this direction," I said.

"How much of a head start did they have?"

"Not much."

"Speed it up." Bix gritted his teeth and banged on the dashboard. "I wish I'd made a run for my own car," he said.

Just then we spotted them. Peyton's yellow Chrysler was three or four blocks ahead of us, weaving a little.

"There!" shouted Bix.

"Okay, if he's taking her home, he has to turn left up there," I said.

Ahead of us, the yellow car wobbled and turned right.

"He's going downtown!" said Bix. "What's he doing that for?"

"He's probably heading for the lake."

"Aaagh," said Bix clenching his hand into a fist.

"I'm just going to keep them in sight."

I turned the corner after them and headed in the direction of downtown. The moonlight was shining on the bleak deserted streets of the warehouse section we were driving through, a sinister setting, I thought. Since I didn't know what I would do if we caught up with Peyton and Celia, I kept a couple of blocks behind them.

"Look at the way he's weaving!" yelped Bix. "He ought not to be driving. Step on it, Katy. Cut him off."

Of course, people are always saying things like that in the movies. Cut him off! Follow that car! Drive him off the road! But it's entirely another thing to do it. I had a certain confidence in my ability to parallel park, but I certainly wasn't up to anything like that.

"What are you waiting for, for Pete's sake! Move it. No, never mind, pull over. Let me drive."

"Be reasonable, Bix. We can't pull right in front of him in my mother's car. We'd end up in a wreck. Now be quiet. I need to think. Turn on the radio. I think better with the radio on."

Bix looked at me blankly. "What are you talking about?"

I glanced at the dash and saw that there was no radio. There had never been a radio. I looked at Bix in horror. "We've got the wrong car! No wonder the key wouldn't fit. We're driving a stolen car!"

In my agitation, I was unconsciously stepping on the gas and soon we were only lengths from Peyton's car.

Bix, seeing them dead ahead, smiled. "Okay, now cut 'em off."

Before we could get into a heated argument about what is the proper course of action when you discover you are following a drunken driver in a car you have accidentally stolen, Peyton's yellow Chrysler jumped the curb, ran up over the sidewalk and thudded to a stop against a warehouse.

Celia got out of the passenger's side and dusted her hands on her long spangled skirt. She seemed to be dressed as Titiana the Fairy Queen or something. A little tiara glittered atop the pale blond of her hair.

I pulled up behind them. "I wonder if Peyton is hurt," I said anxiously.

"He better not be," growled Bix, "because I want to kill him."

Bix tore open his door and leaped out of the car.

Just then, I saw Fuzzy and Mark, in Mark's Studebaker, pulling up behind us. They must have seen us leave the gym and followed us. I ran over to Celia, my bird cage earrings jangling and my flounces swishing like mad. Bix pulled open the driver's side of the car and started dragging Peyton out from behind the steering wheel.

"Are you all right, Celia?" I panted.

"Of course," she said. "I think Peyton's drunk. He wasn't paying a bit of attention to my directions. I kept telling him he should have turned left but he kept talking about going to park at the lake so finally I just grabbed the steering wheel and pulled on the emergency brake." She glanced over in Peyton's direction. "He smells disgusting," she said.

Peyton was propped precariously against the open door of his car and Bix was drawing back his fist.

Celia looked fastidiously away. I was vaguely conscious of a thudding sound and an "Ooomph," as Bix hit Peyton in the stomach, but I had more important things on my mind. Mark and Fuzzy pulled up abruptly behind us and hopped out of the car, Mark in his toga and Fuzzy padded out to the spheroid shape of Humpty Dumpty. Fuzzy's little blue hat fell off and he grabbed for it.

I ran over to Mark, almost sobbing in relief. "Mark!" I said. "I'm so glad to see you. The police may be showing up any minute and listen, this is important." I lowered my voice. "I am driving a stolen car."

Mark blinked. "What?"

"Never mind. We've got to get out of here fast. Get Bix off Peyton."

Peyton was now sagging to the sidewalk and Bix was systematically hitting him. I think Bix was temporarily out of his mind, actually. Mark strode over to them in long steps. "Come on, Fuzzy," he yelled over his shoulder. "This may take two of us." Fuzzy hurried to catch up with Mark. It was very strange to see Humpty Dumpty toddling along next to an ancient Roman in a toga on the deserted, moonlit street.

When the two of them tried to pull Bix off Peyton, Bix was so mad he turned and landed a punch on Mark. Mark yelped but then Fuzzy tackled Bix from behind and knocked him off his balance. While Bix was down, Mark grabbed the chance to sit on him and keep him down. Meanwhile, over by the car, Peyton had sagged unregarded to the ground. He looked kind of sleepy and his musketeer moustache was hanging down, held by only a single thread of adhesive, but evidently Bix had done him no serious damage because a moment later I saw him drag himself up and get back in the car. I even heard a faint click as he locked his door.

Bix, pinioned under Mark, was beside himself with rage. "Get off me, Metcalf. You'll pay for this," he snarled.

In the distance, I could hear a siren.

Celia came over to me. "I wonder if I could have a ride back to the dance?" she asked me politely. She was hugging herself against the chill.

"You'd better go get in Mark's car," I told her.

I could hear Mark explaining to Bix in simple words and single syllables why it was essential we get off the scene before the cops arrived. Finally, the words seemed to sink into Bix's brain and his fury subsided.

"Can I get off you now?" Mark inquired. "Are you quite yourself again?"

Bix laughed. "Get off me, Metcalf."

Bix got up and the four of us sprinted to the blue Studebaker. Mark made a quick U-turn in the street and we headed back to the school, casting some anxious glances over our shoulders as we went.

In the rush to get off, Mark and Fuzzy and I had all crowded into the front seat, leaving Celia and Bix in the back. This was not the best arrangement as I was squeezed in between Mark's bulk and Humpty Dumpty's rotundity, and though I liked being close to Mark, it would have also been nice to be able to breathe freely. With great effort, I managed to turn around. "Are you all right, Celia?" I asked.

"I'm a little shaky, I guess."

Bix looked at her longingly, as if he would have liked to put his arm around her but was afraid to.

"This is a little complicated to explain," I began, "but I think it would be easier if we just forgot this ever happened, don't you?"

"Oh, definitely!" she said.

"What I don't understand is how you and Bix ended up driving a stolen car," said Mark.

"Stolen car?" yelped Celia, sitting bolt upright.

"It was a mistake," I explained. "It looked just like my mother's car and we just happened to take the wrong car in the rush, that's all. It was a perfectly natural mistake. It could have happened to anybody."

"Stolen car?" said Celia again, her eyes wide open.

"Don't worry," I said. "We'll just go back to the gym and act as if nothing has happened. None of us want this story spread all over school, do we?"

Celia shuddered. "No."

I tried to take an optimistic tack. "Peyton might not have even recognized us," I said.

My eyes stole back to Bix, who, dressed as Robin Hood, was not precisely deeply disguised. Not that it mattered. Even if Bix had been decked out in full monster dress with green skin and warty nose, I was sure Peyton would have been able to recognize those fists.

"There was a lot going on," I said, trying to feel hopeful. "And Peyton was probably confused. So I say we just go back to the party and bluff the whole thing out."

It was only when we got back to the gym and began getting out of the car that I remembered the matter of fingerprints.

"May I have this dance?" said Mark as we walked together into the gym and past the bleachers. I felt a twinge of satisfaction when I spotted Mata Hari dancing with a short hobo over by the gym mats.

Mark took my hand and we began dancing to the slow music. I realized that a Halloween dance was not the best place for a person in my excited state of mind. The colored lights hanging from the rafters were casting an odd, unearthly light on everyone. A cyclops with wrinkled, fleshy jowls danced by with a girl in a bunny rabbit suit whose white fur kept changing colors as she danced under the colored lights. A girl wearing dragonfly wings, her thin black antenna nodding gently on her head, strolled by drinking a cup of punch, her face momentarily green when she looked toward us. I shut my eyes to dispel the odd sensation that things around me were getting out control.

"Mark?"

He bent his head to hear me. "What about finger-prints?" I whispered. "What if they find my finger-prints on the steering wheel?"

He squeezed my hand. "No sweat, Katy. Unless you've got a criminal record, they won't have your prints to compare them to, right?"

"Gee, that's right!" I let my head fall back on his shoulder and sighed. There was something very com-forting about Mark. Just leaning against him made me feel calm. Or at least as calm as it is possible to feel while being practically a fugitive.

Chapter Seven

The account of Peyton's accident appeared in the Sunday paper.

No charges have been filed in a one-car accident and a reported assault on North Inverness Road Friday night. Peyton Richardson, Jr., son of Mayor Peyton Richardson, said he was headed north on Inverness Road at about 9:30 when a gang of youths in a white sedan forced him off the road. The youths, whom Richardson described as very big, powerfully built, and dressed in Halloween costumes, then dragged him from the car and assaulted him. No money was taken in the incident.

Police are also investigating the theft of a 1985 white Toyota Corolla found abandoned on the site of the accident. The car's owner, Coach Harvey Mather, said the car was taken from the parking lot of the Hampstead High gymnasium sometime after eight. When interviewed by the *Chronicle*, Coach Mather denied rumors that Richardson had been assaulted by members of the football team. "All my boys were present and accounted for," he said. "This is just another misguided attempt to discredit the fine athletic program we have at Hampstead High. I would like to get my hands on the small but vocal minority of students who engage in this sort of disruptive behavior, and make them eat rice pudding." The Toyota was recovered undamaged.

I put down the newspaper with a shudder. As long as Peyton wanted to give the impression he had been overcome by an army of huge bruisers I didn't see how the description he gave could possibly lead to us. Still, seeing the account of the evening's events in the newspaper did nothing to quiet my mind.

I heard the doorbell and when I went to answer it, Bix was standing on the welcome mat, his hands in his pockets.

"Let's go for a ride," he said. I could tell he wanted to talk so I followed him out to his car and got in beside him. Soon we were driving out toward the deserted roads near his uncle's farm.

"I know I blew it Friday night," he said. "I don't know what came over me." He hit his fist against the steering wheel, and I noticed that the skin was broken across his knuckles.

I felt sad. The truth was that it had been disgusting the way he had kept hitting Peyton. I felt a confused bunch of emotions about it myself and I was his friend. I didn't like to think of Celia's feelings on the subject.

"I don't think you hurt him much," I said. "The paper didn't say anything about his having to go to the hospital."

Bix groaned and I realized I hadn't struck quite the most tactful note.

"And it was his own fault he got so drunk he didn't even try to defend himself," I added.

The look on Bix's face convinced me that I had better give up the attempt to say something comforting.

"Jeez, have I got a problem," he groaned. "I just couldn't help myself. That creep was kidnapping her. I wanted to kill him. But then after I got away from there, I had this kind of sick feeling. You know the way you feel when you've done something bad and there's no way out of it?"

I had a pretty good idea of what he was talking about. Whenever I thought of that stolen white Toyota, I felt that way myself.

"Celia's not speaking to me," he reported morosely. "I called her and she hung up on me. And just when I thought I was starting to get somewhere with her. She apologized to me, you know, back at the gym before everything started happening. She said she was sorry about the way she acted after the concert. But, when she apologized I sort of—well, I guess I wasn't quite as cool as maybe I should have been."

That's for sure, I thought. Of course, Bix did not realize that I had heard every word of what passed between him and Celia.

"I thought I'd try to catch Celia after class and let her know how sorry I am," he went on.

"I don't think it's a good idea. Maybe we should sort of see what develops. I have the feeling we ought to sit tight and wait for things to simmer down," I said uneasily.

The truth was that I was having to admit to myself that my astute understanding of psychology hadn't paid off quite the way I had expected. In spite of all I could do, events seemed to be spinning out of my control. My life as a fugitive had considerably sapped my self-confidence and at the moment I didn't feel up to applying the principles of psychology to the management of people.

Bix kept insisting he wanted to lie in wait for Celia outside her French class when the final bell rang on Monday and tell her how he felt. It was only with great difficulty that I was finally able to persuade him that a hall at Hampstead High that had roughly the at-

mosphere of the Indiana 500 was not the place to ne-
gotiate a delicate affair of the heart. "Give her some
time to cool down before you talk to her," I advised.

I didn't like to come right out and say so, but I was
sure Celia was so embarrassed about what had happened Halloween night that she would chew Bix up
and stomp on him if he so much as looked at her.

It wasn't easy to persuade Bix to let things be for a
while, and I figured it was a major victory that Monday afternoon the whole gang was over at the Bixbys'
house eating Popsicles instead of being busy picking
up little bits and pieces of Bix outside Celia's French
class. I was so relieved I had persuaded Bix not to
speak to Celia just yet that I had for the moment
completely forgotten about the little difficulty we were
having with Peyton, Son of Slime.

Mark was sprawled on the family-room couch
trying to eat two Popsicles at once and having mod-
erate success. "Want to know what the average sen-
tence for grand larceny is in this state, folks?" he
asked.

"No!" I answered.

"We never had adventures like this when Chris was
around," Mark said. "I'll bet she'll be sick that she
missed out. Have you heard from her yet Katy?"

"Just a postcard from the Bahamas," I said. I
would have preferred not to talk about Chris. Nobody had to remind me that Chris had never stolen a
car.

"Don't worry," said Fuzzy, bending his head back to catch a drip from his grape Popsicle just in the nick of time. "They hardly ever catch these joyriders, my dad says."

I leaned the leather recliner back and stared glumly at the ceiling. I noticed that Bix did not have much to say, either.

After a while, Mark burped. "I guess I oughtn't have another Popsicle," he said regretfully.

I dragged myself up out of the recliner. "I'm getting up anyway," I said. "I'll get you one."

I shuffled into the kitchen and opened the freezer compartment. "They're all gone," I called. "Bix, do you have any more of these Popsicles anywhere?"

"Out in the garage. The freezer," he said, not moving from where he was slumped in a big lounge chair. If you had pooled all the *joie de vivre* Bix and I had between us it wouldn't have fueled a microbe's birthday party.

I pulled on my sweater and went out to the garage. In addition to the freezer, which stood in a corner by the workbench, a number of other odds and ends filled the Bixbys' dank garage—a clothesline, a lawn mower, a circular saw, a couple of decrepit saw-horses, a collection of bicycles of various sizes, some cardboard boxes marked Jumble Sale and a Ping-Pong table with a broken net. I suspected a car hadn't been parked in the garage for ten years. Bix's family just stored junk there and left the door open for Bix's younger brothers to play inside on rainy days.

I lifted the top of the freezer and groped for the Popsicles, but my finger encountered something slick that had no coating of frost on it. I opened the freezer wide and took a closer look. On top of the foil packages marked Pork Chops were some plastic envelopes. That seemed odd. Even odder, it looked as if the envelopes were full of dried weeds. I picked up one of the envelopes, examined it carefully and suddenly gasped. It was marijuana! I had seen some only last spring in a drug education class at school and it looked exactly like these dried weeds.

But what was it doing in Bix's freezer? Could this be where Bix's parents kept their private store of the new frozen taste sensation, marijuana-pops? Wait a minute, here, I told myself, getting a grip on my imagination, the Reverend and Mrs. George Bixby were not going to have any private store of illegal drugs in their freezer. Something very strange was going on here.

I dropped the envelope back into the freezer and took the box of Popsicles inside. After I put the Popsicles in the kitchen refrigerator I went to the door of the family room. "Bix?" I said.

Bix's head snapped up suddenly, which is when I realized my voice must be sounding strange.

"Do you know there's marijuana in your freezer?" I asked.

"What?"

Mark began struggling up from the couch. "It's Peyton," he said. "This is chapter two, Peyton strikes again."

I blinked, feeling a little off balance.

"I bet you're right," said Bix. "We'd better hide it fast."

"What about under the carpet?" asked Mark.

"Not so good if they step on it and it goes crunch or something," said Bix. "How much of it was there, Katy?"

"A lot," I said. "I would say Peyton has made a substantial investment in framing you. Money no object."

"Under the couch cushions," said Mark. He lifted one up to reveal some gum wrappers and fifteen cents in spare change.

"It ought to be some place your Mom can't possibly find it housecleaning," I said nervously. "That's the problem."

"The problem is the cops could be coming any minute," said Mark. "We've got to think."

"And Mom," said Bix, growing pale. "She ought to be bringing the twins back from soccer practice any minute now."

I looked frantically around the room. But just when I was beginning to feel my mind was going numb I caught a glimpse, out the glass storm door, of the potted geraniums that Bix's mother had lined up on either side of the back steps. "The geraniums," I said suddenly. "They'll never look in the geranium pots."

All four of us rushed out to the freezer and began gathering up the envelopes of marijuana with both hands. Then, looking as if we were running some sort of eccentric relay race, we all dashed to the back steps. The boys handed the envelopes to me one by one as I sat on the back steps carefully dumping each geranium out. Luckily, the plants were pot bound. Their pots were so filled up with a web of roots that it was easy to tip the plants out and scarcely spill any dirt at all. I folded each envelope of marijuana in half, put it at the bottom of the pot and then replaced the plant. It was unlikely anyone would notice that the geraniums were a little higher up in their pots than before.

"This is really a good idea," said Mark enthusiastically. "You have a natural aptitude for a life of crime, Katy."

I winced. Ever since the affair of the stolen Toyota I had felt a mite sensitive on the subject of crime.

I was sweeping the few crumbs of telltale potting soil off the back steps when we heard a car driving up out front. I let the broom drop on the back steps with a clatter and we all galloped back into the family room and arranged ourselves on the furniture, trying to look nonchalant, as if we had been lazing about there for hours. Bix went to answer the door.

After he left we waited in the family room for what seemed like an eternity.

"Where is Bix?" Fuzzy finally whispered. "Do you think maybe they've arrested him?"

Just then, we heard an engine start up outside, and Mark got up to peer out the kitchen curtains. "They're driving away," he said. "I can't tell if Bix is in the back of the squad car or not."

The back door opened and in came Bix, with a worried crease over his nose.

"We were afraid they had arrested you," I said.

"What are they going to arrest me for?" said Bix. "Possession of pork chops? I'll tell you this—they knew where to look. They walked right on back to the freezer. They had an anonymous tip, they told me." After a pause, Bix added grimly, "Peyton's got to go."

"You're right," said Mark soberly. "He's never going to give up on trying to get back at you. And we can't count on always being this lucky."

Bix fell into a chair. "We've got to think of some way to put that guy out of commission," he said.

I had a momentary vision of Peyton with both arms and legs in casts.

"We gotta think of something real smart," said Fuzzy, looking around at me expectantly.

"Can't you think of anything, Katy?" asked Bix.

I shook my head. I was so relieved to see that Bix didn't plan to go after Peyton with a baseball bat that my mind had gone blank.

Mark went to the refrigerator to fetch another Popsicle. He came back in the family room peeling the sticky paper off thoughtfully. "I know what," he said. "We need a sting operation."

I looked at him blankly. I hadn't the faintest idea what he was talking about.

"Like Bix says, we need to put Peyton out of commission. Fix him for good," Mark went on.

"Would you care to be a little more specific?" I asked. "I don't quite grasp what your nefarious plan involves."

"Simple," said Mark. "We just plant the stereo back on him. That thing is still cluttering up my trunk, you know. Let him explain to his parents why he reported it stolen when he had it all the time. I mean, when you think about it, they've probably already claimed on the insurance. They're bound to wonder what he's up to when they see it's back where it belongs. Next, we plant the marijuana on him. Only we need to do it some way that we're sure it'll be found on him, natch."

"I don't know," I said. "I'm not sure this is right. We don't want to sink to his level."

"Can it be wrong to give him back the very things he gave to us?" asked Mark, looking smug. "Besides, look at it this way. We have a troubled young person here. A young person who drinks and indulges in drugs. Properly looked at, what Peyton has been doing may be seen as a cry for help. Yes, sir, a cry for help. We will help him. Once his problems are brought to the attention of the proper authorities, good old Peyton will get all the help he needs."

I had to admit that Mark had a point. His logic seemed very sound.

"Just how are we going to do this?" I asked.

Mark threw himself down on the sofa and began licking his Popsicle. "I've outlined the grand strategy," he said. "I'll let the rest of you handle the details."

"It's not going to be easy to get the stereo back to him," I said. "To have maximum impact, it ought to look as if the stereo never left his house. It's not as if we could send it parcel post."

"I wouldn't advise burglary. Too risky," Mark said.

"Okay, what would you advise?" I asked, looking at him with exasperation.

He waved his Popsicle airily. "Oh, I don't know. How do people get stereos into houses?"

"Delivery boys bring them," I said, my eyes narrowing as I looked at Fuzzy.

He looked up at me with alarm. "Oh, no," he said.

"We're going to have to case the house, first," I said.

"Katy, the master mind," commented Mark. "That was not sarcasm, Katy, so don't look at me that way. I have faith in you, that's all."

"Bix can't check out the house," I said, "because Peyton might spot him and he'd be sure to get suspicious then." I glanced over at Mark. "Mark can't do it either. He's too big and therefore too conspicuous. And Fuzzy? I don't think so." Fuzzy looked relieved. "I'd better check out the place myself."

"I don't think you ought to do anything that's dangerous," protested Bix.

I thought this was amusing, coming from him, but I said, "I won't. I just want to get an idea of the normal schedule of the house so we can figure out what would be the best time to return the stereo. I'll keep the household under surveillance, that's all." I bit my lip. "It's too bad I've never done any clandestine surveillance before." This was exactly the sort of situation, I thought, in which Freud let you down.

"It's easy," said Mark. "I've seen it all the time on television. First you stroll by, walking a dog. That's how you get your first look. Next you tie a scarf around your head, paint freckles on your nose and ride by on a bicycle. So far, so good. Third, you put on glasses and pretend that you came to read the meter. Nothing could be simpler."

"I don't know," I said. "We're going to have to give this some serious thought."

I was still giving it serious thought when I realized it was time for me to take Caroline to her piano lesson. To my surprise, Bix walked with me out to my car.

"Are you okay?" I asked him when we got to the car. "You aren't upset about what Peyton tried to pull are you? We'll take care of him before he's able to strike again." I got in and put the keys in the ignition.

Bix leaned against my door and sighed, quite unconscious that he was showing his classic profile to advantage. "It's not that. Peyton doesn't worry me. It's Celia. I just can't stop thinking about her."

Bix could have done with a stronger instinct for self-preservation, in my opinion. If he wasn't worried about Peyton, he should be.

But I did my best to be understanding. "I understand," I said.

"I just have this feeling that underneath, in spite of it all, Celia really does care about me. Is that crazy?"

"You may be right."

Bix banged his fist against his open palm. "Then what am I going to do about it?"

I looked at him in alarm. "One thing at a time. First let's fix Peyton."

"I can't keep on this way," he groaned.

I was beginning to see why Mark had said that knights in shining armor were an inconvenience in modern times. Was Sir Galahad well suited to life at Hampstead High? And when you came to think about it, from a practical point of view, people like Romeo and young Lochinvar were equally bad news.

In real life there are some other things that are more important than love—things like getting your homework done and staying out of jail. It would have been helpful if Bix had been able to put his grand passion aside while we dealt with the current crisis.

"Don't worry. It'll all work out," I said.

The problem was, I thought grimly as I drove away, it looked as if it was going to be up to me to make it work out.

Chapter Eight

The first thing I did was to check in the card catalog, first under Surveillance and then under Casing the Joint. No luck. The dumb card catalog prattled on and on at ridiculous length about things no one could conceivably care about, like South Carolina—Description and Travel and Agriculture—the Cultivation of Grapes. But it was a total blank on things a person really needed to know about, like how to put Peyton out of commission.

I would have much preferred some nice electronic method of snooping, something that kept me at a good safe distance from Peyton's house, something like wiretapping or eavesdropping via satellite dish. But that was where I came smack up against the limitations of being an ordinary high school junior instead of a spy for the CIA. I didn't have any wiretapping equipment or satellite dishes. And in that case, Mark's ideas might be the best I could come up with.

After I got back from the library, I looked up Peyton's address in the phone book. Then I coiled my Halloween hair swatch up into a bun, fastened on my head with fifty bobby pins, tucked Dad's reading glasses into my pocketbook and drove over to Peyton's neighborhood. I parked my car about a block away and began strolling ever so casually down Baker Street.

I found that strolling casually was not as easy as I would have thought. I was uncertain about what to do with my hands and it was hard to remember exactly what people looked at when they were out strolling.

When I spotted the mailbox with the name Richardson ahead of me, I stopped abruptly and had to force my feet to keep strolling casually along. Stealing a glance to my left I saw that Peyton's house was a sprawling two-storied white affair. In front, Chippendale planters of yellow chrysanthemums flanked the front door, sitting on a portico with white columns. On the east side of the house another door opened onto a paved patio decorated with more planters of chrysanthemums, and near the patio stood a pretty gazebo of green latticed wood. I noticed approvingly that there was a holly hedge around the whole property and plenty of miscellaneous shrubbery. Excellent for skulking behind, if necessary.

I pretended to be stooping to admire the impatiens planted along the sidewalk near the mailbox so I could get a better look at the house's layout. Just then a woman in a white uniform and apron came out the side door and began beating a dust mop against the steps.

I realized then that only one car was in the driveway, an older blue model with a rusted tail pipe. I couldn't imagine the mayor or his wife driving that car. It had to belong to the maid. Therefore the maid must be alone in the house. This could be important.

Rising, I moved at a fast clip away from the house, feeling very pleased. I had come up with a crucial bit of information on my very first try—Peyton's family had a maid on Wednesday afternoons, and no one seemed to be at home while the maid was working.

The family's absence made psychological sense to me. If someone came in to do the cleaning, you would feel like a worthless bum if you sat around reading a magazine while she was vacuuming your rugs and knocking herself out scrubbing your bathtubs. Better to choose that afternoon to play bridge or do the shopping and avoid the guilt. The day the maid came would be the perfect day for our sting operation.

As soon as I got home, I called Mark.

"Mark! I think we're in business. Nobody's home Wednesday afternoons except the maid."

"Are you sure? Maybe today was a fluke. We'd better check this out again next Wednesday to be sure."

"No, I think we have to take the chance. We can't tell what Peyton's going to be up to by next Wednesday." I did not add that I was a little worried about how Bix was holding up under the strain.

"I don't know," said Mark. "I'm starting to wonder about all this. Maybe it's not such a good idea after all. I mean, it's one thing to kid around about this kind of thing, and it's another thing entirely to skate around close to breaking and entering."

"Quit reading the legal code," I said brutally, "and you won't have such a problem with cold feet. Look at it this way. Do you have any better ideas?"

There was a long silence. Finally, he said, "No."

"It's settled then. Operation Sting is underway."

Actually, it wasn't quite that simple. Bix, Fuzzy, Mark and I spent hours scouring behind liquor stores and grocery stores for boxes that the stereo components would fit in. Next Fuzzy had to arrange to borrow a van from his second cousin, Freddy. Trickiest of all was finding something to make Fuzzy look like a deliveryman. With that daffy grin and that funny mustard-colored hair, Fuzzy just did not look dependable enough to be a deliveryman.

It was Mark that had the inspiration. He checked the yellow pages under Uniforms.

"Uniforms," I said approvingly. "That's very good. The psychologically reassuring effect of uniforms has been well demonstrated in experiments."

Operation Sting wasn't cheap by any means. By the time we put gas in Freddy's van, bought an arrangement of flowers from Garden of Eden Florist and paid for the uniform, we were all bankrupt. But I knew that if we could fix Peyton, it would have all been worth it.

The following Wednesday we helped Fuzzy load everything in the van.

"Now listen, Fuz," said Bix somberly. "This all depends on you."

Fuzzy turned white and gulped.

"You're perfect for it," I reassured him hastily. It was true. We all knew of Fuzzy's genius for looking stupid. And only a deliveryman as confused looking as Fuzzy would be believable in the part we had planned. "There's nothing to worry about," I said.

Fuzzy licked his lips. "I think I better have my dice," he said. "My lucky dice."

Bix and Mark looked at me. I shrugged. "Might be important psychologically," I said.

Bix trotted over to Fuzzy's car and unwound the red dice from his rearview mirror. A few moments later, the dice were bobbing from the mirror of the van and Fuzzy's face had begun to regain his normal color.

"Just remember, be calm," Mark warned him.

"You better not look right at the maid," advised Bix. "Sort of keep your head down and your hat will hide your face. That could be important if something goes wrong."

Fuzzy was beginning to grow pale again.

"Nothing's going to go wrong," I said bracingly. "This operation has all been worked out down to the last detail."

"Right," said Mark. "We've planned it like the invasion of Normandy. What can go wrong?"

"What if the maid phoned in sick?" said Bix suddenly.

"No problem," I said. "I've already checked on that. I called over there a few minutes ago and asked for Mrs. Richardson. The maid told me she wasn't in."

Mark slapped Fuzzy on the shoulder. "There you are, Fuzz. With a brain like that behind you, you can't go wrong, fella."

I'm not sure Fuzzy was convinced. I noticed he was reaching up and frantically fingering his lucky dice as he drove away.

His van had no sooner disappeared around the corner than Bix looked at me and said suddenly, "I can't stand it. I'm going to follow him."

We all ran to Bix's car, piled in and took off after Fuzzy's van. Fuzzy, who was about a block ahead of us, careened around the neighborhood streets at such a pace I was afraid he would overturn the van, but with Bix driving we naturally had no trouble keeping him in sight.

Finally, I recognized the signs we were coming into Peyton's neighborhood.

"Turn right here," I told Bix. "There's a wooded lot behind Peyton's house. We can park there and sneak up behind the house."

We parked Bix's car on the street next to the undeveloped lot behind Peyton's house, then, Bix leading the way, we crept through the pine woods. The twigs seemed to snap like firecrackers as we walked and when we got close enough to Peyton's lot to see the two-storied white house looming ahead of us, I stepped right into a mess of dead vines. "Keep moving," I whispered desperately, tearing at the vines with my fingernails. "Go on. We're going to miss everything."

I tore the last vine from around my ankle and limped to catch up with Bix and Mark. We were making our way right up to the holly hedge that enclosed Peyton's backyard.

"I knew this shrubbery might come in handy," I muttered when we reached the hedge. Moving single file, we inched along the holly hedge where it grew alongside the lot. We passed where the garage loomed huge and white on the other side of the hedge, and then we came up to where we could make out the green roof of the gazebo rising above us. I figured that from there we would have a good view of the side door of the house. It probably wouldn't be safe to get much closer. "Let's stop here," I whispered.

The holly was dense and I was pretty sure the maid couldn't see us. The only danger was that the neighbors might report some suspicious characters slinking in the shrubbery. Fortunately, Wednesday afternoon seemed to be a popular maid's day in Peyton's neighborhood. When we were driving through the nearby streets, I noticed that lots of old cars were parked out in front of the big houses. I only hoped the maids were too busy scrubbing floors or watching soap operas to worry about people skulking through the backyards.

Carefully and slowly the three of us raised ourselves up until our eyes cleared the shrubbery. What we saw was Fuzzy, standing in front of the side door, his arms full of a large cardboard box. The maid stood facing him, her arms folded over her apron. We couldn't hear what Fuzzy was saying but he gestured toward the box and then toward his van parked in the driveway.

The maid bent over to put a triangular wooden wedge under the door, to hold it open for Fuzzy, and he staggered past her into the house with the box. We all held our breath then, but to our relief Fuzzy did not come flying unceremoniously out of the house. Instead, a few minutes later he returned to the van and got another box. One by one, he carried the boxes containing the stereo components into the house. Finally the maid came to the back door to remove the wedge she had put under the door. Fuzzy doffed his hat to her, smiled in his goofy way and backed toward the van.

With an attention to detail that I had to admire, he actually got into the van and began to back it out of the driveway. Next he stopped the van suddenly, threw up his hands in an expression of amazement and disgust that would have been a credit to Marcel Marceau and began to drive the van back up into its original parking place.

Again he got out of the van and knocked at the side door, this time holding out a small bouquet of flowers in a white wicker basket. From our vantage point behind the holly bushes, we watched him mime dismay, apology and disgust. He handed the bouquet to the maid to hold and disappeared into the house.

A few minutes later he came out carrying a box. I personally felt he was laying it on a bit thick about how heavy the box was, but I could understand how anxious he was to conceal that it was now, in fact, empty. One by one, he carried the empty boxes out and loaded them back in the van. Then he politely doffed his hat to the maid, climbed in the van and began backing out of the driveway. We saw the maid shaking her head as she went back into the house.

I grabbed Bix's and Mark's hands. "We've done it!" I said. "By gum, I think we've done it."

"He was good," said Mark excitedly. "I tell you he almost had me convinced that he'd delivered those boxes by mistake."

We crashed back through the wooded lot, leaped into the car and drove to Fuzzy's house, taking the corners chiefly on two wheels. When we arrived at

Fuzzy's house, he was already there, leaning on the van, his cap off, and wiping his moist brow with a handkerchief.

I rushed up to him. "Fuzzy you were great. You're a genius."

He blushed. "It seemed to go all right," he admitted. "I carried them back to Peyton's room like you said. I don't think the maid saw much. She was wasn't too interested until I came in with that bouquet for Peyton. That sort of floored her."

"How did you sign the card?" Mark asked me.

"'From a secret admirer.'"

"That's probably what floored her," said Mark. "She was amazed that Peyton has an admirer."

By now I was leaning against the van, too, limp with relief. I had been pretty sure that everything would go okay, but I was just as glad it was all over. "Let's not forget," I said, "that under Peyton's dippy exterior—"

"Lies a heart as black as a long playing record," finished Mark.

Fuzzy stuffed the handkerchief in his hip pocket. "I need a root beer," he said.

As we moved toward Fuzzy's house, Mark put his arm around my shoulder and burst into "Waltzing Matilda." We were all feeling a little punchy with our success.

Fuzzy's mother was in the carport, squatting down on a vast field of newspaper, refinishing an old chair. She had a smear of brown varnish on her nose and her curly brown hair stood out Afro style around her head. I had never really paid much attention to Fuzzy's mother before, but just then, looking at all that curly brown hair it suddenly hit me why Fuzzy's hair had this funny mustard color. He probably straightened it and then bleached it. It was just overprocessed, not naturally mustard-colored.

"How did your practical joke go, kids?" asked Mrs. Wallace.

"Just great," I told her. "Peyton will kill himself wondering who his secret admirer is." Needless to say we had not told Fuzzy's mother the whole story of our escapade, but some sort of cover story had been necessary.

"I would have thought it would be easier to let the florist deliver the flowers instead of borrowing Freddy's van and the uniform and all," she said, gesturing with the steel wool.

"It was more fun this way," Mark interposed hastily.

Even Fuzzy perceived that a swift change in subject would be best. "We're going to get some root beer, Mom," said Fuzzy. "Then maybe we'll go cruising down Lakeside."

She scoured the chair vigorously with steel wool. "I've never understood what you kids do, anyway, when you go cruising."

"Oh—things," said Fuzzy airily.

"We look at the other kids who are out cruising," I said, "and we stop here and there and get hamburgers and stuff."

"And ice cream at Brendle's," said Mark. "And hot pretzels at Shorty's. And french fries at the fast-food drive-in. And truffles at the candy shop at the mall. And flavored popcorn at Fancy Free."

"Stop, stop," said Fuzzy's mother. "The root beer is in the fridge. The bicarb, should you need it, is in the pantry."

Once we got inside, Fuzzy poured out root beer all around and I proposed a toast. "To Fuzzy," I said, "and to our continued success with part two of Operation Sting."

"Part two?" said Fuzzy, at once looking uneasy. "What is part two going to be like?"

"I'm not sure," I said. "I haven't quite figured it out yet."

Chapter Nine

I had gotten used to Bix showing up unexpectedly at my house when he wanted to go riding and talk about Celia.

"I've been thinking about Celia," he began, predictably, as he turned out toward the country.

"It's been days since we got that stereo back to Peyton," I said, interrupting him ruthlessly. "I wonder what happened."

Bix shrugged his shoulders. "I guess he could have spotted the components and hid them before his parents came home," he said. "Maybe that's why we haven't heard anything."

"Of course, why would we hear anything?" I said. "Peyton could be having horrible, life-threatening scenes with his parents and we'd be the last to know. It's not as if we're his soul mates. We'd be the last people he'd tell about his troubles. It's just that I wish we knew what was going on. It's awful not knowing whether we actually got anywhere with part one of the sting. And if only I could think of what to do about part two! It's bothering me that I can't seem to come up with anything. At night I dream about it and then it seems as if I've found the perfect idea, but when I reach for a pencil and jot it down so I won't forget it, in the morning it turns out to be something really profound like 'The tiger and the mumph.' What do you think that can mean?''

"Dunno." Bix grinned. "Doesn't sound too practical, though. Are you doing the fortune teller tent at the Latin Club fund-raiser?''

"Yes, my fortune telling was such a hit at the Halloween bash that I've been asked to do it again, this time for a dollar a throw. Of course, I've got to think up a new bunch of fortunes since I'll probably get a lot of the same people who showed up at Halloween.''

"Celia's in Latin Club," Bix said, staring at the road ahead.

"I don't think Celia will come to have her fortune told, though," I said. "And even if she does, she'll know who I am so I think she'd suspect something if I told her the stars have destined her to go out with you.''

"I know," said Bix. "But if she does show up, you can put in a good word for me, can't you?''

I grinned. *"Lauda-bo Bix."*

"What?"

"I shall praise Bix. It's Latin."

"You're a good friend, Katy."

"Katy *est amicus magnus*," I agreed smugly.

"Would you cut that out!" said Bix.

I could see that my pidgin Latin could be annoying, but I honestly didn't think it could be any more tedious than hearing about Celia. I didn't say that, though, because I knew even better than Fuzzy and Mark did, how really unhappy Bix was.

He dropped me off at my house and when I walked in the front door, Caroline greeted me with "Woo-wooerwooer," a taunting song on three notes that reminded me forcefully of the third grade and gave me a primitive urge to strangle her. When I noticed her pink plastic locket, however, my annoyance vanished and something in my mind went "Click!" The Answer. I suddenly realized I was looking at the answer.

"Caroline?" I sang sweetly.

She looked at me suspiciously. "What?"

"Where did you get that pretty necklace?"

She covered it protectively with both her hands. "It's mine," she said.

"I know it's yours, dear," I said. "I wanted to know where I could get one just like it."

"At the Toy Mart. Paige Metcalf and me both got one. Some of the girls got the purple ones, but I don't like the purple ones. The yellow ones are yucky, too. Toni Winstead got one and it looks barfy. The pink ones are the best." She pushed on a ridge on the side of the locket with her thumb and it popped open, revealing a shapeless blob of something blue inside. "There's a place inside here for you to put pictures or something, see? Paige and me put our bubble gum in here and then Mrs. Steed can't ever find it, and then we go out behind the trees at recess and chew it."

"Charming," I purred, looking at the locket closely. My subconscious must have been working on the problem all along because now the answer seemed so beautifully simple, so exquisitely clear I couldn't believe I hadn't thought of it before.

I left the house right away and drove to the Toy Mart. There I discovered that Sweetie Pie plastic lockets were one of the biggest ripoffs in modern history at five dollars a locket. I was forced to return home and plead with Mom to give me an advance on my allowance. I was learning that revenge didn't come cheap.

The next afternoon, over at Bix's, part two of Operation Sting swung into action. Outside it was raining and gusts of damp wind were blowing into the garage. I was down on my knees on the cold, damp concrete floor of Bix's garage arranging five Sweetie Pie lockets on spread out newspapers. Fuzzy and Mark were standing on the corners of the newspaper to keep them from getting blown away by the gusts of wind. After I laid the lockets down, I stood back and Bix blasted them with black matte spray paint, and in the process gave a light dusting of paint to the toes of

Fuzzy's sneakers. The lockets dried almost instantly. Then I carefully turned them over and Bix gave them another blast of paint. I knelt down and blew on one, delicately testing its dryness with my finger, then held it up and looked at it critically. "I don't know," I said. "This is not quite it. It needs something."

"I know!" said Fuzzy. "A red hand."

When we all looked at him, he blushed. "You know, like on the sign for Madame Mimi, Palm Reader and Marriage Counselor," he said.

"You know, that might just do it," said Mark.

Bix went over to the cabinet by the work bench and came back with a small jar of red model airplane paint and a paintbrush. "Give me one of them," he said.

I handed over the black matte locket reluctantly. "Just remember, this locket represents a five dollar investment," I said.

He did not answer. Instead, using a brush so delicate it might have been composed of eyelashes, and working with the assurance of an Oriental calligrapher, he quickly sketched some brush strokes on the locket and laid it down on the newspaper for our inspection.

I saw that he had put a small handprint in the lower left of the locket so that it looked as if a mouse had stepped there after playing in a bowl of strawberries. It was amazingly sinister. In fact, it was perfect.

"Darned if it doesn't look as if it actually means something," commented Mark.

"It looks creepy all right," I said.

In less than ten minutes Bix had put tiny red hand-prints on all five lockets.

When he had finished, I put all the lockets in a semicircle on the newspaper so we could admire them.

"Guys," I said with satisfaction. "I think we're in the amulet business."

I had come up with my terrific idea just in the nick of time because that very Friday was the night of the annual Latin Club fund-raiser and the fund-raiser was essential to my plan.

The Latin classes had voted 300 to 50 to have a Saturnalia as their yearly event but Mrs. Phineas knew the students of Hampstead High too well to let herself be swayed by democratic niceties. She promptly overruled the vote. Forestalling efforts of a vocal minority to argue that orgies were an authentic Roman custom that Hampstead High would do well to explore, and soundly quashing an Ides of March commemoration movement that showed all the potential of escalating into a gang rumble, she announced that the Roman fund-raiser would feature instead a fixed-price buffet. The next day we were filled in on the details. It would feature olives, frosted grapes, round bread, salad and baked chicken, with baklava two dollars extra. All members of the Latin Club were expected to attend in costume, i.e. sheets remodeled into togas. For entertainment, the Debating Club would present an oration on rice culture, and Hampstead's orchestral trio, the Ham Heads, would provide music based on a musicologist's reconstruction of what the music of ancient Rome might have sounded like. Lastly, there would be a fortune-telling tent with Cassandra, the seer. Me.

Once Mrs. Phineas outlined the agenda for us, I saw at once that I, as Cassandra, would be the hottest thing going. Compared to an orgy or a reconstruction of Caesar's murder, complete with ketchup, fortune-telling might have seemed dull. But compared to an oration or music that hadn't been on the hit parade since 10 A.D., it was a thrill.

On the evening of the fund-raiser, the little Indian Bob tent was pressed into service again. This time it was set up just beyond all the long tables that had been moved into the gym for the buffet supper.

Outside my tent the gym lights cast a cold, fluorescent glare on the long tables with their white tablecloths and their centerpieces of heaped purple grapes, but inside under the canvas, I had a nice filtered light, quite sufficient for reading the oracles, but not so glaring as to interfere with the air of mystery Cassandra needed.

I had been careful to get to my tent before the rest of the guests arrived in order to protect my mysterious aura. I didn't want Peyton getting a close look at me under the bright fluorescent lights and noticing I was just one of his nondescript classmates.

I was, of course, dressed for the part in a sheet draped fetchingly around me leaving one shoulder bare and fastened at the other shoulder with a rhinestone pin of Mom's.

Instead of the Ruby Lips and Dark Rachel makeup base that Esmerelda the gypsy had favored, Cassandra the seer went in for cold cream and a thick dusting of self-rising flour. I finished off this striking look with broad black bands of eyeliner around my eyes, and lots of mascara. Checking the effect in a pocket mirror on the table in my tent, I put on the final touch. I pinned my hair swatch up near my bangs and let it fall limply down around my face. Cassandra was ready to meet her public.

A few minutes later, when Mark came in to bring me my food and got a look at me, he nearly dropped the plate.

"Good grief," he said. "You look dead. No, I take it back. You look like somebody who died last week."

"Cassandra was not a girl who was full of chuckles, in case you hadn't noticed," I said. "These ancient types were far from jolly."

"Well, you don't look jolly, so you must be on the right track." He sat down and put a paper plate filled with food on my little round table. "I got them to let me back in the kitchen before they put out the buffet so I could get you a plate," he said. "I was afraid you wouldn't have time to eat once they start serving. People might start coming back to the tent right away."

I picked up a chicken leg and began gnawing on it. "Thank you. That was very thoughtful of you. Yes, I also have this feeling that Cassandra will be very popular. Have you seen Peyton yet?"

"Relax. I spotted him a minute ago. It was lucky for us that Mrs. Phineas decided to give extra credit for this do or I'm not sure he would have shown up. Think about it—when's the last time we've seen that yellow Chrysler of his cruising along Lakeside? He's getting to be a regular hermit."

"Good," I said. "Maybe he's been grounded because his parents have found out about the stereo. That will only make this part of our plan that much more effective."

I finished the chicken leg, dried it carefully with a napkin and put it in my red cardboard cylinder.

"What are you doing with that chicken bone?" said Mark, looking uneasily at the empty paper-towel tube I had painted red and recycled for use as a bone cup.

"It's a part of my fortune-telling kit," I said, shaking my collection of bones out on the table so he could see them. From Sunday's dinner I had saved a rather nice wishbone as well as a couple of shiny wing and thigh bones and now I had the drumstick as well. An impressive collection. "I figure Cassandra predates crystal balls," I explained. "She probably read chicken entrails and bones and stuff instead."

"I'm glad you didn't go for the entrails."

"There's such a thing as carrying authenticity too far," I agreed.

Outside, I could hear the trio tuning up. At least I thought it was tuning up. It may have been the music because what followed didn't seem that different from what went before.

"I'd better scram," said Mark.

"What? You don't want to hear your fortune?"

He settled back onto the stool.

"Unbeliever," I clucked, flashing him a reproach-ful look. I shook my chicken bones out onto the small round table and looked at them.

"From his toenail one may tell a lion," I intoned in my spookiest voice. "Cassandra sees your nature. She sees that you are a lover of cakes and sweetmeats, a lover of pleasure and song." I delicately lifted the chicken leg, replaced it in the cylinder and rattled it for added effect. "The ending crowns the deed. Proceed with wisdom and kindness and you will be called most fortunate."

Mark grinned and folded his arms. "You're good at this," he said.

"You don't think it's too bland?" I asked.

"You can always throw in a few cries of 'Woe be-tide! Woe betide! I see blood!' And then, of course, you can warn the Christians to steer clear of lions."

It was only a couple of minutes after Mark left that my first customer made her way into the tent. It was Marnie Nichols, president of Latin Club. I noticed right away that the safety pin holding her toga at the shoulder had worked its way undone. That could be useful.

I shook the chicken bones and tried to avoid letting my eyes steal up to Marnie's safety pin. It was still stuck through the layers of material, but it definitely was not fastened.

I held my hand to my forehead. "Falling!" I cried. "I see falling!"

Marnie's eyes were wide. "Not my grades, I hope," she said nervously.

I peered at the bones. "I think not your grades. This falling is before the night is out. Take care! Oh, take care! Not all our power lies in mind and body and even steel may fail us." I held up a finger in front of my lips and whispered, "Remember, time bears away all things."

"Gee," said Marnie. "Do you mind if I take notes? It's a little hard to drink this in all at once."

"Not at all. All us oracles tend to be on the sibylline side. That will be one dollar, please," I said. I took the bill from her hand and stuffed it in the mayonnaise jar at my feet.

"Do you by any chance have an enemy you would care to zap?" I inquired. "We have a special enemy amulet, a limited offer only, for fifty cents. You wear it for two weeks to get the desired effect."

Marnie looked interested, but cast a nervous glance behind her. "Nothing too bad would happen to her, would it?" she asked. "My enemy, I mean. I wouldn't want to get into anything really heavy."

"Let your mind be at ease. These amulets are USDA inspected."

"Just a little light suffering, huh?" She chuckled fiendishly. "I'll take one." She fished two quarters out of her pocketbook and laid them on the tablecloth before me. When I gave her the amulet, she held it in her palm and looked at it with admiration. "Neat!" she said.

"Remember, you must wear it for a week."

"I thought you said two weeks."

"That's right. Two weeks. One week for the regular blight and two weeks for the extended warranty."

Marnie smiled happily and backed out of the tent, my first satisfied customer.

She was immediately followed by Peyton. He had wasted no time, that was for sure. I noticed that the flesh around his eyes now looked only light yellow. The twin black eyes were almost completely gone. He was definitely in better shape tonight than he had been Halloween. His hair had a look of plastic perfection, he was wearing a perma press toga, and he looked almost alert. He sat down on the stool and leaned over the table to get a closer look at me. "You know, you sort of look like that gypsy. Same little bitty nose. Are you two related?"

"Distantly," I said, backing away from him.

"She was good," he said. "Let me tell you. She said I'd be taking a journey and there'd be a lot of confusion and maybe some danger and I mean to tell you, she was right on the money."

Thinking it best to avoid further talk about the gypsy, I quickly shook the bones out on the table. Peyton seemed a little startled, but he was obviously interested.

I peered at the wishbone, then threw up my hands, taking care not to tip over the tent as I did so. "Woe!

Woe!" I cried. "Night pitch-black lies on the deep. Arising from the bones I see an avenger of wrongs."

"What are you saying?" said Peyton anxiously. "It doesn't sound too good."

"There is but one hope," I said. "Hope not in safety."

"When do we get to the good part?" said Peyton with a nervous laugh.

"Well, I do happen to have this amulet, available only as an introductory offer for our first five customers and guaranteed to bring trouble to your enemy. Only fifty cents."

Peyton groped desperately under his toga for his pants pocket. "I don't think I have fifty cents left."

"We take Mastercard," I said quickly.

"Wait a minute," said Peyton. "I think I've got it after all." He fished out four dimes, a nickel and five pennies and laid them out on the table.

I gave him the amulet and then reverted to my spookiest voice. "You must wear this amulet around your neck for two weeks," I said, "in order to have the full benefits. Fail not!"

Peyton held it in his palm and looked at it in fascination. "How about that!" he said. "This thing really socks it to your enemy, huh? Does it protect you, too? I mean protect you from your enemy?"

"I cannot say. Even Cassandra does not fully understand the powers of the black amulet."

"What's this funny little red hand?"

I lowered my voice. "Only those of the Brotherhood of the Red Hand can answer that question." I made a gesture of farewell. "Go, my child. Cassandra's bones have spoken."

Peyton backed out of the tent looking like a cat that had been given free run of the aquarium.

"Piece of cake," I murmured as soon as the flap of the tent had closed.

I only had one misgiving. I hoped Peyton had enough sense to take off the dumb thing when he showered. If black matte started flaking off to reveal Sweetie Pie pink underneath, we would be in the soup.

It was hard to keep my mind on my next few clients, but the remaining three amulets went quickly. It seemed that everybody had at least fifty cents worth of enemies.

I must have done about fifteen fortunes when all at once I heard a shriek not far from the tent followed by sounds of confusion. My second sight told me that Marnie's safety pin had at last lost its grip.

Moments later Bix pushed the flap open and handed me a glass of grape juice. "Mark told me to bring you this. He thought you'd be getting thirsty." Bix said this in the tone of one for whom hunger and thirst had little interest. "Did you hear all the screaming out there? Marnie Nichols's toga bought it."

I felt a swift rush of guilt. I had got so caught up in being Cassandra that I had forgotten that nice Katy Callahan would have told Marnie about that slipping safety pin.

"Is she okay?"

"Oh, sure. She just grabbed up the sheet right away and wrapped it around her. Then she took off for the bathroom with about a hundred girls following her. I think they all had extra safety pins." He reflected a moment. "Pretty slip she had on. Any luck with Peyton, yet?"

"He was hot off the mark. He was my second customer. And he took the bait but good."

Bix lowered his voice and bent close to me. "You're sure you gave him the right one, aren't you?"

"Don't worry. I kept his amulet in my pocketbook, separate from all the rest in the shoe box. There was no chance of a mixup."

Bix ran his fingers through his hair uneasily. "Any sign of Celia?"

"No," I said, shooting him a sympathetic look. I could have told him that Celia was not the type for fortune telling. Anybody who worked as hard as Celia didn't need to worry about luck. "Don't worry, Bix. She'll calm down. And after we get this business with Peyton taken care of, I'll go and talk to her."

"I've got an idea," Bix began.

"Tell me later. You better get out of here. The customers in line are going to get restless. Thank you for the grape juice."

"Okay," said Bix, backing out of the tent. "Talk to you later."

Chapter Ten

Sunday afternoon, Mom was going with Caroline to *Peter and the Wolf*, but she dropped me off at Brendle's on the way. "When you're ready to come home, dear, give Dad a call. He ought to be finished with those reports anytime now. But if you don't get him at home, try the office."

"Don't worry, Mom," I said. "I'll have one of the guys give me a ride home."

Except for Fuzzy, Mark, and Bix, who were sitting around a little white table, Brendle's was empty since it was not exactly the high season for ice cream. The white wire ice-cream chairs with their heart-shaped backs and their pink cushions looked oddly out of season silhouetted against the lowering gray of the skies outside the big windows. I picked up a single scoop of chocolate, carried it over to the table and squeezed in between Mark and Fuzzy.

Bix was helping Mark eat his banana split, an unheard of eventuality. I wondered if Mark was nervous about the part he was to play in Sting II. Fuzzy, I noticed, was demolishing a chocolate float with unimpaired appetite.

"Nothing to it, Mark ole boy," Fuzzy said cheerfully. "You've just got to keep your head. You know, be cool, look natural."

Mark put down his spoon and looked at his banana split with distaste.

"To tell you the truth," he said, "I'm not sure I can pull this off. Maybe somebody else had better do it."

"We've been all over that," I said patiently. "You and I are the only ones who have a class with Peyton, and since I'm the one who gave him the locket it would look fishy for me to be the one to do it."

"Phys. Ed.," Mark said suddenly. "You've got Phys. Ed. with Peyton, don't you Fuzzy? I remember you told me about how Peyton puts all that gook on his hair after he showers."

"The plan won't work in Phys. Ed.," I said. "There are too many people, too much confusion for it to be effective. It's got to happen in Latin class, Mark. We don't have any choice. But I promise you it's nothing to worry about. All you have to do is bump up against

Peyton as if you're losing your balance and then hook your pinky around those plastic beads the amulet is hanging from, until you break it. You'll be fine."

Mark heaved a sigh. "I don't have the nerves for this kind of work."

Fuzzy looked complacent. "It does take nerve," he said. "Nerve like cold steel." He slapped his hand on the table and all the ice-cream dishes rattled. "Guts. That's what it takes. I wish I could do it for you, Mark ole boy, but I just don't happen to take Latin."

I ignored Fuzzy. "You're perfect for this job," I told Mark in a soothing voice.

"Big, you mean," said Mark bitterly. "Big and clumsy. If I knock Peyton over nobody will think anything about it. There he goes again, clumsy Mark."

I had never seen Mark in such a black mood. He had me worried.

Bix squirmed uncomfortably in his chair. I suppose he was conscious that he was the one who had gotten us into all this and that so far he was the only one who hadn't been able to help out. He cleared his throat. "If Mark doesn't feel up to it, maybe we can work out something where Peyton and I are called to the office at the same time and then I could do it."

"Nah," said Mark, stirring his ice cream disconsolately. "Won't work. Peyton won't let you get close to him, if he can help it. I'll be okay, Bix. Don't pay any attention to what I've been saying. I'm just getting a case of cold feet. I'll be okay tomorrow."

Fuzzy slapped him on the back. "Don't worry about it, Mark ole boy," he said. "You'll be great."

Mark looked down at the banana split as if it were the condemned man's last meal. "Sure," he said.

We ran over a few last-minute details, then I announced that I needed a ride home. "Can somebody give me a lift?" I asked.

"Sure," said Bix and Mark simultaneously.

Then Bix said, "No, really. I'll do it. I need to go by Katy's house anyway to—to borrow a book."

I could see that Bix wanted to talk to me about Celia so I resigned myself to riding home with him though it was a sore disappointment. I had really been hoping for a few minutes alone with Mark to sort of buoy his confidence and let him know that I really believed in him.

We all walked out to the parking lot together. Mark's sad, bloodhound eyes followed me as I got into Bix's car. I felt like a total crumb. I rolled down the window and waved to him. "You'll be great!" I cried. "I know it."

He got in his car without answering.

As Bix pulled out on Mulberry Avenue, he wasted no time in getting to what was on his mind. "I've been thinking of this thing with Celia," he began.

"I'm worried about Mark," I said. "He looked actually sick back there. Did you notice he didn't even touch his banana split? Maybe we ought to put this business off until he's feeling better."

"Don't worry about old Mark," he said with brutal cheerfulness. "He always comes through on the day. He'll be okay. Look, like I said, I've been thinking about this business with Celia. I've been watching the way you work, Katy—cool, calculated, with a plan. And I admire it. I mean, heck, it's going like gangbusters. By tomorrow afternoon, we'll have Peyton wrapped up with ribbon and ready to ship off. Now what this makes me think is that what I need with Celia is a plan. A plot, you know? A scheme. You're not the only person around here who can have an idea." He grinned.

"What kind of idea do you have?" I inquired uneasily.

"We ought to make her jealous."

"That's dangerous," I said promptly. "Besides, I don't think we ought to do anything until this Peyton business is wrapped up. One thing at a time."

"I'm tired of waiting," Bix burst out in an anguished voice. "I haven't been doing anything but waiting and waiting. I called Celia up last night and she acted as if I were selling magazine subscriptions. I can't take it anymore. Now listen, it's not as if we can help Mark with Peyton. He's on his own now. No point in us sitting around holding our hands. We might as well be doing something useful. Now, aren't you always saying I should act as if I don't care about Celia so much?"

"Ye-es," I admitted with some hesitancy.

"All right. If I start seeing somebody else, then I'll look cool, right? She'll start having second thoughts, maybe."

"Maybe," I said, brightening a little. "Why not?" It had suddenly occurred to me that it would be a good thing for Bix to see other girls. It might help give him a sense of proportion and it would certainly keep him out of my hair. I was not going to have any peace of mind until after sixth period tomorrow when Mark finished his Peyton gambit and it would be nice to have Bix out chasing girls until then and staying out of my way.

"There's just this slight problem," he said.

"Don't go telling me nobody will go out with you," I said, "because I don't believe it."

"No, that's not the problem." He looked embarrassed. "The problem is that most girls, if you go out with them they get all soupy and start falling apart. It gets embarrassing. They start calling you up at home. You can't get away from them."

There was something odd about this, I realized, in a grisly sort of way. I had the feeling it hit on something very basic about the way the universe worked. Bix was telling me that most girls turned him off because with the slightest encouragement they fell for him. Celia's indifference to Bix had probably been what interested him in the first place. But now it was Bix that was soupy and Celia who was turned off. If this was the way human relationships worked, it amazed me that anybody ever got together at all.

"Well, let's forget it then," I said promptly. "To tell you the truth, it's a risky idea, anyway. I wouldn't advise it."

"I think it would work if you'd be the girl."

"Me!"

"I'm not asking much, Katy. We'll just stage a couple of scenes to start Celia thinking that maybe I've started noticing other girls. That's all."

"What kind of scenes?" I asked, aghast.

"A kiss, a hug, no big deal. I've got it all figured out."

"No," I said.

"We could do it between second and third periods in A building. Celia will just be coming out of chemistry and she'll bump right into us."

"No. I think it's a rotten idea."

"Look it is not a big favor I'm asking. And don't you remember you said you'd be happy to help me out with Celia after the way I taught you to drive?"

It was true that had it not been for Bix my means of transportation would still be limited to bike and trike, but I was not sure it was sporting of him to remind me of it.

"And you like me okay, don't you?"

"Sure. I guess so." I was not so sure of that as I had been a few minutes before.

"So what's the big deal about a kiss?"

"Celia's not going to like it," I said.

"That's the idea." He smiled.

"It's not honest," I said.

Bix snorted at the idea of letting such a piddling objection stand in the way.

"Also, I have a bad feeling about it," I said. "Look, Bix, can't we just talk about this after tomorrow? You don't seem to realize that I've got a lot on my mind right now."

"You don't seem to realize what this means to me," he countered. "How much time can it take? Five minutes? Five lousy minutes of your time."

"It's not the time I'm worried about," I muttered.

I couldn't believe it, but I let Bix talk me into it. It went against my better judgment. It would be embarrassing. Furthermore, as I pointed out to Bix, it could possibly be physically dangerous because there was a good chance that anyone pausing for a kiss between classes at Hampstead would get trampled in the general stampede. Even the strange people who chanted mantras between classes had the good sense to do their chanting at a fast trot.

Bix argued that was what made his plan such a good one. Since kissing in the halls was so unusual, it would really catch Celia's eye.

I am not sure, but I think I finally agreed just to shut him up. I had reached the point that if I heard the name "Celia" one more time my sanity would be seriously threatened.

But Monday morning, when Mark picked me up for school, it was a toss-up which of us looked the sickest.

"Are you okay?" I asked, when I saw his face. "You don't think you're coming down with anything, do you?"

"Nope," he said.

"Because if you are feeling sick, we can always put this off a day or two."

"I said I would do it, didn't I? Did Bix get his—book all right?"

"Huh? Oh, yeah, sure." I suddenly had the feeling in my stomach that you have when an elevator goes down too fast when I was reminded of Bix and his plan.

Obviously, a person who had any strength of character would never have let somebody talk him or her into something against his or her better judgment, I told myself. What would Mark think if he found out I had let Bix talk me into this? He would think I was a weak-kneed little idiot and he would be right.

"You aren't worried about how I'm going to do with this thing, are you?" asked Mark, swallowing and looking rather pale. "Because I practiced it ten or twelve times with Fuzzy pretending to be Peyton and I think I can do it."

I reached for his hand and squeezed it. "I know you can. You'll be great."

This did not cheer Mark up any. If anything, he looked sicker than before.

First and second period seemed unusually long, but at last, checking my watch, I got up and told Mr. Hatchard I had to go fix my contact lens. Instead of fixing my contact lens, of course, I went to meet Bix outside Mr. Benson's chemistry class. We had to be sure to get into position before the bell rang in order to be sure that Celia would see us.

"You're a sport, Katy," Bix said, putting his arm around me. I was annoyed to see that he was looking very pleased with himself.

"You don't have to start until the bell rings," I said tartly.

Just then the bell exploded with its usual nerve-shattering noise and people began pouring out into the halls. Bix drew me closer, looked into my eyes and kissed me while around us hundreds of people thundered past. At first, I was surprised nobody bumped into us, but then I remembered how everyone at Hampstead took particular care not to run into Bix.

Then we drew apart. It hadn't been so bad, I was thinking as he drew away. Nobody had trampled us. I had lived to tell the tale. We both looked toward Mr. Benson's class. Celia and Mark were standing just outside Mr. Benson's door, frozen, as if in suspended animation. Then suddenly they looked down and hurried away.

Bix broke into laughter. "Did you see that?" he asked. "Metcalf thinks you and me were making out! Did you get a load of his face?"

"Exceedingly funny," I said coldly.

"Celia definitely looked shook, don't you think?"

"Quite possibly," I said. I had already decided I would never forgive Bix as long as I lived.

He slapped me on the back. "That's what I like about you, Katy. You don't get all soupy."

I had never dreamed that Mark was in Celia's chemistry class. I wished I could have run right over to him and explained. I couldn't *wait* to explain. Unfortunately, first I had to go through third, fourth, fifth and sixth period. Particularly sixth period.

"Now today, class," said Miss Hayes as soon as the sixth period bell had rung, "we will review the special and irregular comparison of adjectives for Tuesday's quiz."

The truly beautiful thing about Miss Hayes was that she was absolutely predictable. That was what made her so boring as a Latin teacher but so perfect for my plan. She always asked people to put conjugations on the board on review day and she always began with the first people on each row. This meant that Peyton and Mark would be getting up to go to the board at the same time, which was crucial.

I held my breath, hoping that Miss Hayes would not decide to take some new and original approach on this day of all days.

"Alan," she said, "please give us the positive, comparative and superlative forms of *facilis*. Peyton, do the same for *liber*. Mark, please take *pulcher*. Jason, will you give us *acer*, and Barry, give us *bonus*." She looked up at the board thoughtfully. "I think that's all we have room for right now," she said, as if she hadn't said the same thing every Monday since Noah was hammering nails into the ark.

"Could I switch places with you?" I whispered to Marcy Dotson. "I can't quite see the board."

Giving me a startled look, Marcy moved her notebook back to my desk and I moved up into her desk, closer to the action.

Peyton was dragging himself up out of his seat with the lack of enthusiasm of someone for whom the comparative forms of *liber* were some of the darker mysteries. Seeing that Peyton was dragging his feet, Mark dropped his pencil to gain time, all the while casting nervous glances over at Peyton, who was slowly rising from his desk.

As soon as Peyton was on his feet, Mark got up and charged blindly over in his direction, colliding with him. Peyton let out a sound like "whoof" as the wind was knocked out of him. Quickly Mark reached out to Peyton's shoulder as if to steady himself, caught his hand on Peyton's black-beaded necklace and then stumbled again. The string of tiny beads broke and the amulet came crashing down to the floor.

The clasp, in the time-honored fashion of cheap plastic, immediately broke and the locket was flung open. "Look what you've done!" Peyton shrieked hysterically. "You've broken it!"

The pink interior of the locket lay open to view now and the marijuana we had planted inside was partly spilled out and partly stuck to the locket because it had been slightly damp from its stay in the flowerpot when we pressed it inside.

Miss Hayes was absentmindedly checking Alan's construction of *facilis* on the board.

I saw at once that I was going to have to take a hand or foggy brained Miss Hayes would never even notice the marijuana. Peyton was already getting his breath back and was struggling up again from his desk. It would be only a matter of seconds until he scooped the locket up and the evidence would be gone.

"Goodness!" I said loudly. "It's marijuana! I mean, isn't that marijuana? It looks just like that stuff I saw in the drug education slides last year."

Mark stood in front of Peyton, as if by accident, blocking him from getting up, while everyone stared at the shattered locket on the floor and the dried leaves spilling out of it.

Miss Hayes dropped her Latin book, hurried over to the locket and looked down at it suspiciously.

"It's just herbs or something," said Peyton. "The Brotherhood of the Red Hand put it there, probably."

Miss Hayes sucked in her breath with shock, no doubt imagining that the Brotherhood of the Red Hand was our local branch of the Mafia. She quickly recovered, however, and reaching for a manila envelope from her desk she carefully scooped up the locket and its contents on a sheet of paper, put it in the manila envelope, licked the flap and sealed it.

"Hey! What are you doing?" yelped Peyton.

"I'm afraid I shall have to confiscate this material, Peyton, until an investigation can be made." She then signed her name on the flap of the envelope, making me wonder if our mild-mannered Miss Hayes had a part time job as a police stool pigeon. She seemed to be effortlessly gearing up to testify in a court of law.

"You can't do that!" said Peyton.

Miss Hayes looked at him over her glasses. "You are mistaken, Peyton. It is my duty to do that." She folded the manila envelope, put it in her purse and snapped the clasp shut. "Now, who can put the positive, comparative and superlative forms of *facilis* on the board for us?"

The class was buzzing with excitement and from then on the positive, comparative and superlative forms put on the board were pretty much a hash. I don't know what Peyton's state of mind was, but by the time the final bell rang, I was practically a stretcher case. The way Miss Hayes had signed that envelope in such an official way had given me the creeps. It had suddenly hit me that I might be called to testify in the case. Of course, I had realized that I would have to be in a position to show that I had given out other lockets and that all the others were empty. I had bought five of the lockets just to cover that eventuality. But testify? Perjury? Or, just as bad—the truth? I felt definitely sick.

I hurried to the parking lot, eager to talk to Mark in privacy. But when I went to the parking place where we had parked the Studebaker that morning, it was empty. At first, I had the odd feeling that I must have forgotten where we had parked. But then I remembered that there was no such thing as an empty parking space in that lot. I hadn't gotten the parking spaces mixed up, Mark had just left without me.

"Katy!" yelled Fuzzy. I spotted him one row of cars over. "You're supposed to ride home with me," he called. "Mark had to go straight home."

I went over and got in the car. "Is Mark sick or something?" I asked. "Why did he have to go home?"

Fuzzy shrugged. "Dentist or something. I don't know. He put a note on my locker. 'Take Katy home,' it said." As we pulled out of the parking lot, Fuzzy lowered his voice and asked eagerly, "Well, how did it go?"

I leaned back in the seat, feeling weak. "It went just the way we planned."

He laughed. "Boy, would I have liked to see Peyton's face. I'll bet he looked sick."

I didn't see how he could have looked any sicker than me. After Fuzzy let me off at my house, I ran inside and called Mark, but it rang and rang and I got no answer.

I jumped in the car and drove at once to Bix's house. "Bix," I said in an awful voice when he came to the door, "you go find Mark and tell him that kiss in front of chemistry class was just a joke, do you hear me?"

"Good grief, Katy, what's the big deal?"

"Don't argue. Just do it."

"Hey, are you and Mark—"

"He's not answering the phone. I don't even know where he is," I said, wringing my hands.

"Probably off somewhere stuffing his face," said Bix.

I realized at once that Bix was probably right, but his tone did not endear him to me.

"Well, find him!" I ordered. "And tell him I really need to talk to him. Oh, Bix, I'm so worried!"

"Calm down," said Bix, closing the door behind him and coming outside to talk to me. "How did the business with Peyton go?"

"Just the way we planned. That's what I'm worried about. Look, we're wasting time. You go find Mark. I'm going home."

The hour I spent at home waiting was one of the longest hours of my life, longer even than when my braces were put on, longer than when I was waiting to say, "I am calcium and I build strong bones" in the second-grade nutrition play. But at last, when my eyes were practically dry from continually staring out the living room window, Mark's blue Studebaker pulled up out front.

"Bye, Mom," I yelled, grabbing my jacket on my way out the door. "I'm going."

"But I'm about to put supper on," she protested.

"I'm not hungry," I said. I ran out the front door and over to Mark's car. I didn't wait for him to invite me, I just opened the door and got in. I sat there a moment, hyperventilating, while Mark looked at me in a funny way. Finally he said, "Bix said you needed to talk to me."

"Oh, Mark," I sobbed. "What if they call me as a witness? I could be convicted for perjury. Or something worse. Didn't you notice how Miss Hayes signed that envelope? That's because she wants to be able to testify in court that the contents truly are the same that she picked up off the floor in Latin class."

He patted me on the back awkwardly. "Don't worry about it, Katy. The case'll never come to court."

"How can you be so sure?"

"A tiny bit of pot like that? And with all the pull Peyton's dad has in this town? Give me a break. Peyton'll just be quietly shipped off to some private school that specializes in rich juvenile delinquents. I promise."

"You really think so?"

"Yup." He started up the car. "Want to go get some hot pretzels?"

"Yes. Yes, I do."

He turned the car north in the direction of the mall. "You know, I thought you and Bix had something going there. Caroline kept telling Paige that Bix was your boyfriend."

"Caroline will shortly be put up for adoption," I said grimly.

"I was having some trouble believing it," said Mark. "It didn't seem to square with everything else, somehow, but then when I came out of chemistry class, I was, well, surprised."

"Celia was the one that was supposed to be surprised."

"Yeah. That's what Bix said."

"What a day," I groaned. "What an awful day."

"I don't know what it takes to please you," Mark said, the corners of his mouth twitching. "You frame Peyton, you put the positive, comparative and superlative forms of *felix* on the board with only two mistakes and you get kissed by the best-looking guy at Hampstead High and you're still not happy."

I groaned again. "I'm giving up plotting. I have no interest anymore in managing human behavior."

"What you need is a hot pretzel to restore your self-confidence."

"You think that will do it?"

"It always works for me," said Mark.

Sure enough, just as Mark had prophesied, I slowly began to feel less and less as if I were going to have a nervous collapse. The next day Peyton quietly disappeared. We later heard he was enrolled at St. Matthew's Military School.

When Bix called Celia that night, she burst into tears and said she wasn't getting any work done and would probably never get to be one of the first three chairs in the Allstate Band. Bix offered to come over and help her concentrate and Wednesday afternoon I saw them walking towards the parking lot holding hands.

When we spotted them, Mark looked over at me a little uncertainly as if wondering how I would feel about this development. I couldn't believe he could be in any doubt about it, but I was beginning to realize that Mark had this strange idea that he wasn't attractive. Possibly it came from years of catching glimpses of himself in shop windows standing next to Bix.

I got in the Studebaker and closed my door. Mark slid in behind the wheel. "Isn't it great to see Bix and Celia together at last?" I said. "I can't tell you what this means to me."

Mark started up the ignition. "You know," he said, "this gypsy told me that a charming girl was going to be absolutely crazy about me. I didn't know whether to believe her or not."

"It's a mistake to brush off what gypsies say," I said. "You know, those crystal balls, the wisdom of the East. They know things."

"Yeah," he said ruefully, "but all the time she was talking I kept thinking how big I am. And clumsy. And slow."

I giggled. "You're slow, anyway. That's for sure."

He leaned over and kissed me. Through the windshield I caught the startled gaze of Marnie Nichols. I suppose she had been one of the hundred or so people who had seen Bix kissing me on Monday. Ah, well, I thought, leaning back in the seat with a contented sigh. If anybody asked, I would just explain that my irresistible charm was due to a special deal on an amulet that I had gotten from a gypsy. One thing I had learned was that people will believe absolutely anything.

* * * * *

Read more about Katy and the gang in Love and Pizza to Go by Janice Harrell, coming next month from Keepsake.

COMING NEXT MONTH
FROM
Keepsake

KEEPSAKE # 11
LOVE AND PIZZA TO GO
by Janice Harrell

The old gang from THEY'RE RIOTING IN ROOM 32 is back again. Once more they're into trouble, adventure and romance.

KEEPSAKE # 12
THE MYSTERY KISS
A Blossom Valley reissue
by Elaine Harper

Who stole a tantalizing kiss from Polly Anderson on Halloween night? She would just have to find out!

AVAILABLE THIS MONTH

KEEPSAKE # 9
THEY'RE RIOTING IN ROOM 32
Janice Harrell

KEEPSAKE # 10
THREE'S A CROWD
Brenda Cole

COMING NEXT MONTH
FROM
CROSSWINDS™

SHOCK EFFECT
By Glen Ebisch

Being a waitress in a summer hotel can be more than just hard work, as Monica found out when she discovered a corpse in a bedroom. Was it murder?

KALEIDOSCOPE
By Candice Ransom

Cress and Darien find that life is a mysterious design of changing patterns. After initial misunderstandings, they decide to explore it together.

AVAILABLE THIS MONTH

THE EYE OF THE STORM
Susan Dodson

BIGGER IS BETTER
Sheila Schwartz

Did you hear about the war on flab?

My flab! Well, my mom, who's a gorgeous movie star, decided she couldn't have a fatso for a daughter. So she tried all kinds of stuff. Do I need to tell you that NOTHING WORKED? I didn't get skinny, I just got mad. And when I get mad, watch out....

Bigger is Better

SHEILA SCHWARTZ

Coming from Crosswinds in October